Away with the Fairies

J. McKeaveney

authorHOUSE®

AuthorHouse™ UK Ltd.
1663 Liberty Drive
Bloomington, IN 47403 USA
www.authorhouse.co.uk
Phone: 0800.197.4150

Published by AuthorHouse   05/14/2013

ISBN: 978-1-4817-9445-9 (sc)
ISBN: 978-1-4817-9446-6 (e)

To

Auntie Akash

with love

from

Joanie

xxx

I would like to acknowledge Mary McWilliams for her expertise in editing this book, which was essentially one long paragraph full of bad spellings, little punctuation and questionable tenses. While Mrs McWilliams did an excellent job of correcting the hard copy, the author was less diligent in making said corrections. Therefore any errors are entirely the fault of the author and not the editor.

I would also like to acknowledge the inspiration provided to me by my parents who were both avid readers and instilled in me a love of reading and writing. They also believed enough in me to help pay for the publishing of this book which is much appreciated.

I feel that I must also acknowledge some of the sources of my inspiration (which cannot go unnoticed by anyone reading *Away With The Fairies*). *Gone with the Wind, Wuthering Heights and Jane Eyre* have all been read so often that I can barely speak without quoting from them. They are great works of literature and I know I am being extremely presumptuous even mentioning them in the same paragraph as my own little work, but I can't help it. They now form part of my psyche and are my friends.

Finally, I would like to mention that, while none of the events or people depicted in *Away With The Fairies* are true, I have been provided throughout my life with an array of inspirational characters, friends, family and anecdotes which have influenced the writing of this novel.

THIS BOOK IS DECICATED TO
MY MARKIE

Chapter One

Rosie Maguire was a bit of an eejit. In her own head she was destined for greatness; in reality she was much less significant. To anyone who knew her well, Rosie was the epitome of chaos. She could enter a tranquil scene of every day domesticity and turn it into a war zone within seconds. Equally she could enter a wake house and leave the mourners laughing. Fortunately, for Rosie, she was spared the insight of knowing she was an eejit. Being seventeen she was never wrong, and could not understand the endless litany of complaints and accusations that were levelled at her by her elders and betters. If anyone had a problem it was definitely not Rosie: sure she was *great craic!*

Rosie was sitting in Mass beside her family. It was July, and the chapel was hot. The sermon was particularly long that day. The younger children fidgeted in their seats, while the babies either slept or cried. The rest of the congregation were genuinely involved in the mass. They were good people and their faith was important to them. For Rosie, her Catholic faith provided enough encouragement to keep her behaviour on the right side of the law; though it failed miserably to quiet her restless soul. Nor was it able to provide Rosie with the equanimity required for a meaningful existence. Rosie did not wish to miss out on *eternal life,* but she struggled with the technicalities of her religion. The restrictive and often sexist nature of the Church did not sit easy with her. Characteristically Rosie had managed to find a loop-hole that, she believed, allowed her to sin with relative impunity. She attended Confession once a month, where she would list her latest misdemeanours and obtain absolution from the priest. She would then walk away feeling renewed, smug in the knowledge that she alone had figured out how to make religion work to her advantage.

Rosie's favourite pastime was daydreaming. She spent considerable amounts of time in a state of semi-consciousness: suspended between the world she had created in her mind and the reality of her, rather insular, existence. Mass was the perfect place for Rosie to indulge her favourite hobby. Her internal musings were interrupted periodically by the need to sit, stand or kneel, according to the ritual of the Mass. Rosie was able to do this automatically; with only the occasional nudge from her mother to remind her to move appropriately. Most of Rosie's daydreams where centred on one person: Jim O'Loan. Though Jim had never spoken more than a couple of words to her, Rosie believed herself to be deeply in love with him. The subject of Rosie's desire was sitting three rows in front of her in the chapel. He was unaware of Rosie's devotion to him. He was only just aware of her existence. Rosie studied the back of his head. He had a gorgeous neck. She wanted to touch him but he was beyond her reach. It was just as well. Sometimes when Rosie was deep in thought she did things without being completely conscious of her actions. If Jim O'Loan had been sitting right in front of her, chances are she would have been unable to stop herself from reaching out to stroke him. Rosie willed Jim to turn around and look at her. He appeared to be listening to what the priest was saying. Rosie rarely listened to anything figures in authority had to say. In situations where concentration was required, Rosie was incapable of paying attention for more than a few minutes. The sound of the priest's voice only served to lull her further into her dreamlike state. Her thoughts flickered about until she settled on a single subject. She had just finished re-reading *Gone with the Wind* that week. Inevitably she began to dream about being Scarlett O'Hara, southern belle and main love interest of Rhett Butler. Rosie's imagination often carried her away to distant lands and bygone eras. She was happier there: no one could get her.

Rosie sighed deeply. *Is it really possible for any human being to possess a seventeen-inch waist?* She wondered. Rosie's mother heard the sigh and glared at her daughter. Rosie adopted a look of extreme piety and bowed her head, as if praying. After a moment she looked up to see if her mother was still cross. Mrs Maguire was saying her prayers and was no longer watching. Rosie glanced at her family. She had two younger sisters and two younger brothers. She also had an older sister called Anne. Anne sat quietly in her seat and appeared to be listening to the priest. Rosie's younger siblings looked bored and Ryan, who was only eleven, was clearly asleep. Suddenly everyone in the chapel stood up. As if sleepwalking, Rosie stood up too and repeated the *Our Father* in unison with some two hundred other voices. Just as suddenly everyone sat down again and Rosie resumed *praying*. In Rosie's opinion Scarlett O'Hara was an incredibly silly young woman. For Rosie there was never any comparison between Ashley Wilkes and Rhett Butler. Had she been Scarlett she would have married Rhett instantly, and made him very happy. They would have had many babies and grown old together. Frankly, Rosie was *herself* a very silly young woman. She was only vaguely aware of the disharmony she caused amongst her family, and could not comprehend the almost obsessive dislike she engendered in some of her teachers. As a child she had attempted to reason with bad tempered adults but, over the years she had developed less time consuming, and more effective, ways of dealing with their unreasonable behaviour. Generally she denied or lied her way out of most confrontations.

When Mass was over, Rosie decided to walk the mile and a half home rather than be seen in public with her four younger siblings and her older sister Anne. They were such an embarrassment. The fight to get a seat in the car without a smaller child on your knee usually resulted in an argument that lasted longer than the journey home. Rosie did not want to be seen with her family. The local lads always stood at the entrance to the chapel grounds and watched the girls coming out. Jim O'Loan was usually in the centre of the group. He was a natural born leader and the others were happy to bask in the reflected glow of his charisma. For Rosie, the walk from the chapel door to the gates, produced a heady mix of emotions, ranging from anticipation, to deflation or elation depending on whether or not Jim spoke to her. She lived in hope of the day that Jim might actually do more than nod at her.

Apart from living in hope, Rosie lived in Tullybeg, a small, rural community beside the southern shores of Lough Neagh. It was 1984 and, while Northern Ireland was a country divided by *The Troubles*, Tullybeg was a quiet, peaceful place to live in. It provided a haven of tranquillity that contrasted sharply with the political and social upheaval in the country, as a whole, at that time. It also contrasted with the unholy emotions that permeated the soul of Rosie Maguire. For Rosie, the real life substitute for the sweeping hills and red earth of *Tara*, were the decidedly smaller, greener, and in winter time, muddier fields of Tullybeg. It was summer time now and the country side was at its' best. Rosie loved the simple beauty of the landscape, but she despaired of its isolation and remoteness.

Kate, Rosie's younger sister, who was nearest in age to her, being sixteen, wanted to walk home too. Rosie was not amused. Competition was not in her best interest. Kate was a natural beauty, taller and slimmer than Rosie, with long, chestnut coloured hair and exquisite bone structure. They both had hazel green eyes, but Kate had perfectly shaped eyebrows, delicate pink cheeks and a rosebud mouth. Rosie was darker and shorter. Her skin was generally brown, but she had red cheeks that flashed when she was excited or embarrassed. She also had an infectious laugh and considered herself to be extremely witty. Kate was more feminine, demure, and decidedly better dressed. Rosie never seemed to get herself organised in time to dress well. Usually she just borrowed clothes from her sisters to wear. Invariably Mrs Maguire ended up refereeing a screaming match whenever the item of clothing was returned stained, torn or stretched. Rosie glanced down at her ensemble of the day: jeans and a boy's shirt. Kate wore a pretty, ankle length pinafore dress which Mrs Maguire had made for her. She had copied the design from a dress modelled on a mannequin in *Top Shop* in Belfast. Kate looked lovely. Rosie resigned herself to walking ahead of her so that any potential *talent* would see her first and hopefully ignore the vision that followed.

Rosie waited with Kate outside the chapel doors, until her parents, Anne, and the younger Maguires had driven off. Rosie did not wish her mother to see her talking to boys. She needn't have worried. As she sauntered past the assembly of teenage lads waiting at the wall she got no more than three nods and two brief 'hiyas' from the group who were straining to catch a glimpse of the *vision*. Kate smiled, but did not speak, as she followed Rosie out of the chapel and down the road home. Jim was talking to an older man as Rosie passed; he had not seen her. Rosie's heart sank as she realised it would be another week before she saw, let alone spoke to, him again. She lapsed into silence as she began to trudge home. Kate followed behind her. As the two girls walked along, they gradually approached a lone figure who was ambling slowly ahead. He had evidently left Mass before the end of the last hymn. Rosie recognised the figure of Sean O'Loan, Jim's older brother. There were five brothers in total: Sean was the eldest and Jim the youngest. The O'Loan family lived on the other side of the *Wee Lough* which the Maguire family home looked on to. The *Wee Lough* or Lough Tully as it was properly named, was a small expanse of, virtually stagnant, water that was hidden from general view by the hills surrounding Rosie's home. The Maguire family had a perfect view of the *Wee Lough* from the back of their house. From their kitchen window it was just possible to see the roof of the O'Loan house on the other side of the water.

Rosie felt uncomfortable walking behind Sean, but dreaded the thought of overtaking him and having him walk behind. Rosie was acutely aware of her figure and felt that her she was not shown to her best advantage from behind. Sean O'Loan was twenty-four years old, five years older than Jim. Therefore his opinion was not worth anything: being decrepit as he was. However, given his status as Jim's elder brother, he was worthy of acknowledgement. Rosie decided to speed up and overtake him. Kate had no say in the matter as she was younger and clueless when it came to strategies in relation to men. When the girls were almost parallel to Sean he turned around and said,

"Hello Miss Maguires!"

Kate looked at him without any difficulty and offered a polite, yet warm,

"Hiya Sean!"

Idiot! Thought Rosie, *you don't just say hiya to an older man, you have to say something more grown-up.* Rosie asked about Sean's mother, who had not been well, in the most sophisticated voice she could muster. Sean smiled wryly at her and said,

"Oh, I think she'll live Rosie. What about yours?"

"Oh, grand" she said, eager to get to the point of the meeting,

"and the rest of the . . . family?" she continued.

Sean noticed her hesitation. He thought for a brief moment, then replied,

"Jim's OK Rosie. Did you not see him at Mass?"

This time Sean spoke with a blatant grin on his face. He was teasing her. Rosie's face immediately coloured at the mention of Jim O'Loan's name, and at Sean's obvious knowledge that she fancied him. She was mortified at the thought that Sean might tell Jim that she had asked specifically for him, when she very clearly had not!

"I wasn't looking for him" stammered Rosie, before turning her back on Sean and attempting to walk on. Kate interrupted the awkward silence that followed by asking Sean about work. For once Rosie was glad of her younger sister's presence. Sean fell into a natural, warm discussion with Kate about the amount of work he had on at that moment. Sean's entire family were in the building trade. He spoke with authority while managing not to sound patronising. Rosie walked in silence, slightly behind the pair, until they came to the turn in the road leading to Sean's house. He said goodbye to Kate before turning to Rosie,

"I'll tell Jim you were asking for him then Rosie" he joked.

"You needn't bother!" she snapped, before turning on her heels and storming off. Kate apologised to Sean for her sister's rudeness, but he only laughed and waved goodbye.

When Kate and Rosie arrived home, breakfast in the Maguire household was well underway. Sunday breakfast was always superior to the weekday affair. Fried bread, tomato sauce, sausages, bacon and eggs was the norm. Rosie kept one eye on her own plate and the other eye on everyone else's plates. If there were any left-overs she was first to *bags* them. Rosie loved food. She occasionally worried about putting on weight, but being extremely active it was never a real concern. After breakfast the usual fight about who was doing the washing-up ensued. Even though it was not

Rosie's turn she opted, in the end, for doing the breakfast dishes so she would be free after dinner to do her *own thing*. Rosie chatted to her mother while she cleaned up. Mrs Maguire was already starting to prepare for dinner which was generally served at two o'clock. She listened to her daughter with a bemused look on her face, occasionally interrupting the chatter to give Rosie domestic directions. Rosie was an efficient house keeper but she was also incredibly clumsy. She was known for spilling, dropping, breaking and losing things. Her sisters hated lending Rosie anything as it was unlikely to be returned. If it was, it was returned in bits. Rosie had very few prize possessions. The only things she valued were her books. These were a motley collection of novels and classic literature stolen or *borrowed* long-term from the school library and from other people. Her mother frequently reminded her 'never a borrower or a lender be'. The latter part of this instruction was easy for Rosie to follow, as she rarely had anything worth lending. However, she was like a magpie when it came to 'borrowing' other peoples stuff. Anne had placed a life time ban on lending Rosie anything. Anne was meticulous about her own possessions. She still had all her childhood books, dolls and keepsakes tastefully displayed on her *side* of the bedroom which she and Rosie shared. Rosie's side of the room was a disaster zone. Clothes and shoes lay on the floor where they had been discarded after wearing. Dog-eared books and magazines were piled high beneath the bed. Items of make-up and *borrowed* jewellery clung precariously to the top of the overcrowded dressing table, frequently spilling into the open drawers below. Whichever *project* Rosie was working on at the time took pride of place on the middle of the unmade bed. Every Friday after school, Rosie made a half hearted attempt to clean up prior to her sister's arrival home form university. Anne had first gone off to Queen's University in Belfast the previous September and, despite the fundamental differences in their personalities, Rosie missed her elder sister very much and looked forward to her coming home at weekends. She was deeply in awe off Anne's superior status in the world. Anne was an adult and was relatively independent. She shared a flat in the city with friends but still came home every weekend. To Rosie this was the height of sophistication and she could hardly wait to achieve the same goal. She desperately wanted to go to university and live in a flat in Belfast. She wanted to travel. Anne was planning a month's holiday in Greece, island hopping with her best friend. Rosie could not contain her jealousy.

After finishing the dishes, Rosie retired to her bedroom to finish the book she had been reading. Anne was lying on her own bed deep in thought when Rosie burst into the room and flung herself on the bed.

"What ya doing?" she asked.

"Studying" replied Anne.

"Aye, right you are Anne! You're near asleep there" said Rosie laughing, "you just pretend to be studying to get out of doing dishes, you lazy sod!" Anne stared at her in mock horror and asserted that she was, indeed, contemplating an assignment she was 'just about to start'. Anne was a compulsive worrier and was *actually* trying to decide if she could justify spending half her student grant on a holiday when she would be left living in debt for the rest of the year. Like the three youngest Maguires, the eldest Miss Maguire had copper coloured hair and deep brown eyes.

With magnolia skin and a flawless complexion Anne cut a fine figure of a woman. She was however, unlike Rosie, deeply averse to the male species and considered them all to be idiots. A feminist through and through, Anne's main objective in life was to embark on adventures abroad which would involve her in death defying feats of valour and self-sacrifice, ultimately resulting in her gaining fame and fortune without having to *go out to work.* She reasoned that this would allow her to live independently for the rest of her days. As a career choice Anne figured her plan was flawless. Rosie continued to snigger as she grabbed her book from under her pillow. She decided to leave Anne to her *studying* and finish her novel. *Wuthering Heights* was Rosie's favourite book of all time. She was re-reading it for the thirteenth time. While Heathcliff lacked the overall appeal of a man like Rhett Butler, he was by far the sexier of the two, and Rosie could not help wishing she lived on the moors in close proximity to a man like him. She was convinced that, had she been Catherine Earnshaw, SHE would never have allowed herself to die and would, in fact, have ended up marrying Heathcliff and having babies. This was Rosie's main objective in life, after a suitably long *forenoon,* in which she would break several hearts and generally have fun at the expense of a string of suitors.

Just as Rosie was getting to the really good bit, when Catherine is dying, Ryan came running into the girls' bedroom and announced,
"Barney's lost!"
Although he was too old to cry, Ryan was visibly distressed. Barney was the family's pet dog and was loved by all. He had joined the household when Rosie was eight and, in dog

years, he was now quite old. Rosie loved Barney, but was not overly concerned at the news. She had spent many hours looking for Barney in the past, only to have him return of his own accord after he had sown his wild oats, or finished some adventure with a new friend. Ryan, however, was frantic so Rosie set her book down and agreed to help him look for the lost dog. They both went outside and started to call the dog's name. Ryan trotted behind Rosie as she made her way onto the road and turned right into the lane leading down to the *Wee Lough*. They called continually but Barney did not appear. After some twenty minutes Rosie ordered Ryan back to the house to see if he had returned from the opposite direction.

"Call me if you find him, Ryan!" Rosie shouted, as Ryan went running back to the house, "I'm going down to the *Wee Lough*".

"Righto!" Ryan answered, as he disappeared through the hedge at the back of their home.

Rosie followed the overgrown lane which led to the field that bordered Lough Tully. The field was on a hill. When Rosie reached the top she was able to look down and out across the small stretch of water. She could see cars driving on the road at the other side of the Lough and, in the distance she could see the roof of the O'Loan family's house. A gentle breeze disturbed the grass and tugged at her shoulder length hair as she scanned the landscape looking for the little dog. Barney was so short it would be impossible to see him if he was in the hay fields. Rosie called his name several times, but to no avail: Barney did not appear. She wandered down to the waterside avoiding the tall reed like grass which indicated that the ground was not as it seemed. Lough

Tully flooded the neighbouring fields in winter time. Often the ground was treacherously boggy well into the summer months. Rosie remembered that she was wearing Kate's new canvas slip-on shoes. She looked down at them and realised in horror that they were already covered in grass stains and mud.

"Oh, shit!" She exclaimed out loud. Immediately she heard a concerned male voice ask, "Are you all right Rosie?"

Rosie turned around and saw Jim O'Loan approaching quickly, reaching his hand out to offer her assistance. Rosie was startled and stepped back at the sight of him. Unfortunately the canvas shoes were not made for trekking through uneven ground. Rosie caught her foot in a hole, lost her balance and fell backwards onto her bottom. The ground behind her was wet, sticky and muddy. Jim O'Loan immediately ran forward to help her. He was wearing *wellies* and was able to stride through the mud with relative ease. In two swift movements he had Rosie on her feet and back on safe ground. Rosie was mortified. She could feel the cold, slimy sensation of mud clinging around her backside and sliding down her legs. One of the canvas shoes remained in the hole; the other was covered in a black watery mess. Her hands were also covered in mud where she had reached back to try and save herself. Without speaking Jim guided her to a nearby tree stump where he told her to sit down. He then retrieved Kate's shoe from the bog and placed it on the ground beside Rosie.

"I don't think you'll be wearing that again Rosie" he said. Jim looked so concerned that Rosie could not help but smile and reassure him that they were only an old pair of shoes that she was going to throw away anyway. He remained concerned for her loss until Rosie lifted the shoe and flung it as far she could into the water. They both laughed when they heard the shallow splash. Rosie then removed the other shoe and it went the way of its twin.

"You're mad, Rosie Maguire!" Jim exclaimed, as he sat down on the tree stump beside her. Rosie was instantly aware of the odour of his body next to her. He smelled of *Lifebuoy* soap and fresh sweat. Jim had just tramped through several swampy fields. He had been walking his own dog, a Springer Spaniel named Finn. He called to the dog now and gave a sharp authoritative whistle. From a distance of two fields away Finn's ears picked up and he came bounding back to his master within a matter of seconds. Following behind was the lost Barney who waddled as fast as his little legs could manage. He looked surprised, and then overjoyed to see Rosie. She scolded him for being so far from home; then patted and kissed him until he shook with pleasure.

"I was looking for you, you stupid mutt" she said, as she caressed the little dog. Jim watched her. He was aware that they were alone and unseen. He was aware of the long grass and he was acutely aware of the sensations arising in his young strong body. He wanted to touch her. He had seen Rosie Maguire a million times before and thought she was pretty. He had never considered her though as a potential girlfriend. Kate was the real beauty in the Maguire family and nothing but the best would do for Jim. Now being close to her, he could feel the life force brimming in her. The sight of her covered in muck, shoeless and smiling, with the glow of physical exertion on her face made her suddenly very attractive to him. Rosie was acutely aware of the proximity of his body. He was leaning into her as she straightened her body and turned to face him. He gazed at her but said nothing. Rosie's face coloured instantly.

Her hands were filthy and she did not know where to put them. She wanted to stand but was afraid to move. She was exquisitely uncomfortable and her head was filled with a thousand possible things that she might have said at that moment. What she chose to say was,

"I need to go to the bathroom." The words filled the air like a sudden shower of rain. Rosie stood up instantly and stammered, "I mean, I need to wash my hands . . . . they're covered in muck."

Jim stood up too. He knew she was embarrassed. He smiled and said,

"So's the rest of you Rosie."

Rosie looked down at her clothes and bare feet. She was a sight. She wanted the ground to open up and swallow her. Jim thought she had never looked so lovely.

"Come on," he said, "I'll walk you home."

They both called to their dogs and proceeded to the brow of the hill. At the top was a gate. Rosie was about to climb over when Jim reached for her. He scooped her up in his arms and planted her over the hedge onto the firm ground on the other side of the gate.

"Don't want you falling again, Rosie", he said, by way of explanation. Rosie's heart raced. She wondered how much she weighed. She now realised the benefit of having a seventeen-inch waist and, for the first time in her life, bitterly regretted having her huge Sunday morning fry for breakfast. Jim then jumped over the gate and ordered the dogs to follow by way of a hole in the hedge. The physical contact with Rosie had unnerved him too, but outwardly he remained unshaken. He wanted to touch her again; without hesitating he reached out and grabbed her mucky hand as if it was a natural and regular occurrence. He then continued to walk along the lane. Having taken her hand he was unable to look at her face. He was worried that he had misjudged the situation. He wondered if she too was longing to be touched. For her part Rosie was in a trance. She was walking beside Jim O'Loan and he was holding her hand as if it belonged to him. *Oh heavenly event!* She sighed to herself.

They reached the back of the Maguire's garden which had no proper entrance. It was accessed by a large gap in the hedge, and a plank placed across the drain which ran along the back of the property. Rosie was glad that Jim had not gone to the front of the house as all eyes would have been upon them. He turned finally and looked at her. She gazed up at his face. He had pale green eyes and long dark eyelashes that any woman would have given her eye teeth for. Rosie was unable to talk. Her heart thumped and her hands began to sweat through the dried on layer of mud. Jim gazed back at her. He slowly reached forward and touched her on the cheek before tilting her chin up and kissing her firmly on the mouth. *Yes,* thought Rosie, who felt like shouting for joy and doing a victory dance on the spot. Jim smiled at her warm response to his kiss and the obvious joy on her face. She was not the most subtle of creatures. He liked that about her. So often he had taken girls out for the night and had been left wondering, at the end of the evening, whether they even liked him. Girls that played games or *hard to get* were stressful to be around. Jim was never sure what they expected or wanted and a date usually proved to be more a battle of wits than a fun night out. Jim had indeed been out with his share of girls who were willing to throw themselves at him. He had known girls whose sexual experience was as much a pressure as it was a magnate. He was no saint but there was part of him that just wanted to be with a girl who he could relax with and who made him feel good. Rosie was looking at him now with her large, appreciative eyes and he felt very good.

"Well I suppose I better go Rosie and let you get your dinner" he said.

"OK Jim, thanks for kiss . . . oh, I mean for . . . helping me . . . I mean for . . . good bye!" Rosie stammered. Jim smiled at her embarrassment. His heart swelled at the idea that she should be so in awe of him.

"Rosie, can I see you again?" Jim asked, as Rosie was about to disappear though the gap in the hedge. She turned slowly to him and immediately said,

"Yes." Rosie was not worried about sounding too eager. She was worried that he would change his mind or disappear or that she would wake up.

"I'll call you during the week then" he said.

"The number's in the book" she replied, before calling for Barney and running away through the under growth. Jim turned away too. For the first time in his life, he was excited about seeing a girl again.

Chapter Two

Rosie ran up to the house, Barney following behind. They were both mucky, and out of breath, when Rosie burst into the kitchen where Mrs Maguire was engaged in preparing Sunday lunch.

"Josephine Mary Maguire!" she exclaimed, "What in Hades have you been at? . . . and where are your shoes?"

Rosie suddenly remembered that she had thrown Kate's lovely new canvas slip-ons into Lough Tully. She was in need of an urgent, instant lie to get her self out of trouble. *This is going to be really difficult* she thought, as she slumped down on one of the kitchen chairs, preparing herself to be creative with the truth.

"You see Ma it was like this," she began, "Barney was lost, and I walked down to the Wee Lough to see if he was there, and sure enough, he was playing in the water . . . . but when I called to him to come out he got stuck in the mud, and I had to go and rescue him! But didn't I get stuck too, and I fell, and Kate's shoes got lost, and I had to walk the whole way home in my bare feet . . . but isn't it great that I found Barney?"

18

Mrs Maguire stared at her. Rosie could not face her mother. Mrs Maguire always knew when Rosie was lying because she could not make eye contact.

"You mean you were wearing Kate's new shoes!" exclaimed Mrs Maguire in disbelief. She knew Rosie was not telling her the whole truth, but could not think of any reason why her daughter would have voluntarily fallen in the Lough and covered herself in mud and lost her sister's shoes.

"Rosie, you are so careless. Why on earth didn't you change those new shoes before you went looking for that stupid dog?" Mrs Maguire's question was reasonable. Rosie knew that she had not given any consideration to Kate's new shoes or to Kate, who had been kind enough to lend them to her, after Rosie had begged her for an hour that morning. Rosie felt guilty, and whenever Rosie felt guilty she became defensive and offensive at the same time. She stood up instantly and, looking just above her mothers eyes, she exclaimed indignantly,

"Mummy I was nearly drowned in the Wee Lough and I saved Barney's life and all you can think about is a pair of stupid shoes." Rosie turned on her heal and stormed out of the kitchen banging the door behind her. Her mother sighed in frustration. There was scarcely a door left in the Maguire household that hung properly on its hinges. Mrs Maguire decided that the best punishment for Rosie was to let her face the wrath of her sister Kate. She would also have to pay for replacing the shoes. They cost £5.00 in *Dunnes Stores*: as Rosie only earned £10 a week at her Saturday job this was would be devastating. While Mrs Maguire went on with peeling potatoes, she looked out of the kitchen window and across the fields to the top of the hill which bordered Lough Tully. In the distance she saw the figure of a tall man, walking with his dog. Mrs Maguire stored information like that in the back of her mind. With four daughters she had to be, if not one step ahead at all times, at least no more than one step behind.

Meanwhile Rosie was in the bathroom getting washed and changed. *What on earth am I going to tell Kate?* she thought, as she rinsed muck from her feet and hands. She decided that the best ploy would be to distract Kate's attention by telling her about her recent romantic encounter. After getting dressed she went into the bedroom which Kate shared with their youngest sister Orlagh. Kate was tidying up. She had not forgotten about lending her shoes to Rosie but, before she could enquire as to their whereabouts, Rosie launched into her tale about meeting Jim O'Loan on the hill beside the Lough.

"Guess who I just ran into?" Rosie began.

"A wind tunnel?" replied Kate, looking at Rosie's dishevelled hair and red face.

"Very funny Kate" retorted Rosie. "No, in fact," she paused for dramatic effect, "Jim O'Loan!" Kate was suitably impressed and the two girls sat down on the bed, in true conspiratorial fashion, as Rosie described the recent events to her sister. She did not mention the bit about losing Kate's shoes. For her part, Kate asked all the right questions. Details were shared about the kiss and the girls giggled about who would be bridesmaids at the wedding and how many babies Rosie and Jim would have. Kate was genuinely pleased for her sister as she had listened to Rosie talk about Jim O'Loan for the past three years on a daily basis. As Rosie got up to leave the room the inevitable question was asked by Kate,

"By the way Rosie, where's my shoes?" Rosie froze in her tracks.

"Ah, you see Kate, it was like this . . ." she began. The argument that followed lasted till after dinner. Mrs Maguire chaired *proximity talks,* and it was eventually agreed that Rosie would indeed pay for a new pair of shoes from her weekly wages. Kate finally agreed to forgive her sister, and Rosie was glad to have the whole thing over with so she could get back to day dreaming about Jim.

After dinner it was Anne's turn to do the dishes. Mrs Maguire was lying down in the living room watching the Sunday afternoon film with Kate and Orlagh. It was *Calamity Jane,* one of Rosie's favourites, but she did not want to sit in the living room. Things were still a bit tense between herself and Kate and she was definitely not *flavour of the month* with Mrs Maguire. Rosie went out side to the back garden. Her father and two brothers were outside. Mr Maguire was gardening, while Ryan cut the grass. The eldest boy Conor, who was fifteen, was sitting on the garden bench. He was patting Barney who snuggled beside him. Rosie squeezed in beside them and patted Barney too. The wee dog was in heaven with his two favourite people sitting next to him.

"What you at?" Rosie asked Conor. She was not particularly interested in anything her younger brother had to do but she was bored now, and Rosie did love to talk just for the sake of talking. Conor was a lad of few words. At least, at home he did not say much. Amongst his peers he was regarded as a fun loving, easy going fella. Amongst his predominantly female family, he considered the least said the better. Women were definately a breed apart and, his highly strung and unpredictable older sisters made no sense to him whatsoever. He was very protective of his younger sister Orlagh, but the thought that his older sisters might ever need protection did not occur to him. They were all formidable personalities and, to be frank, he felt sorry for any man who might dare to interfere with them. He considered his reply carefully before answering Rosie,

"Not much. What about you?"

"I just got a bollicking for losing Kate's shoes. You know it wasn't even my fault," replied Rosie.

"I heard" said Conor, who had been aware of the argument even though he was outside at the time. He empathised with Rosie. He too was renowned for losing and breaking things and, like Rosie, he was always horrified at the anger directed at him whenever he messed up. After all, it wasn't as if he did these things on purpose. Conor believed that people set too much store by worldly possessions. He had long since decided that, as soon as he was eighteen, he would head out into the world with a rucksack on his back and the price of a one way ticket to Thailand. He intended to live life to the full, and experience freedom in a world devoid of authority (and sisters).

Conor was almost six feet tall already and was still growing. Technically he could have made life very difficult for the girls in his family, but his father had instilled in him a reluctant respect for the *fairer sex*. He had inherited the belief that woman should be spared the harsher realities of life. When he was eight years old his father had woken him up on Christmas Eve night in order to help him finish making a dolls house for Orlagh. As he helped his father paint, Conor realised that girls and boys were different. It was not for him to reason why but to work with his father to appease the wrath of five women in one household. The enormity of his situation was brought home to him on a daily basis as he watched his sisters grow more unreasonable and, in his opinion, increasingly psychotic everyday. They were known as the *Mad Maguires*, and at times it pained Conor to be associated with them. It would be many years, and two long-term relationships, before Conor would begin to understand the role PMT had played in his adolescent development. As sure as the waxing and waning of the moon were the monthly *mega fights* in the household: when at least one, if not two or three, of his sisters would reveal their true identities and become *harpies from hell*. It was on these occasions that Conor questioned his father's attitude to his daughters. It was difficult for him to see that any of the women in his family (apart from his mother) deserved to be treated with respect when they were threatening to disembowel him and each other. His psyche was to be eternally traumatised by the sight and sound of their ear piercing screaming matches which lasted for hours at a time. At the moment however, Conor was happy enough to chat with Rosie. She could be quite humorous at times and it was a case of *anything for a quiet life*.

"I think I'll go into town on the bus and see Ellie" said Rosie, standing up, wiping dog hairs from her jeans.

"Tell her I said hello" said Conor. Ellie was Rosie's best friend who had just turned eighteen. Shane was old enough to know that an eighteen year old girl would not be interested in him as such, but he was young enough to dream. Ellie had a very good figure and large bust. Whenever Conor met her he could not take his eyes of her chest. Ellie had known the Maguire family for ten years. She had stayed in their house frequently and was considered an *honorary* sister.

Ryan was afraid of her, as she had often scolded him along with his sisters. Ellie was, however, fond of Conor and had acted as mediator in more than one family argument when Conor was being verbally lashed by the *Harpies*. Rosie said cheerio to Conor, gave Barnie a final pat on the head, and ran off into the house to ask her mother if she could go to town.

Mrs Maguire was still irritated with Rosie, but the film had put her in better spirits. She loved *Calamity Jane* too and, when Rosie asked if she could go into Tullymore to see Ellie, Mrs Maguire could think of no valid reason to say no. Her general rule was to say *NO* first to most requests from Rosie. This allowed her time to try and ascertain what motive Rosie had for any of her actions. On this occasion however, Mrs Maguire felt that everyone would benefit from a Rosie free environment for a few hours. Rosie ran off to wash her hands and face and to spray some deodorant on. She only wore makeup if she was going out for the evening so her preparations for town were short and sweet.

Tullymore was the nearest large town and was about five miles from Tullybeg. On Sundays there were only three buses running into Tullymore from Tullybeg; one in the morning, one at about three o'clock and one at six o'clock in the evening. Rosie had just heard the 3 o'clock bus go down the road towards Tullycross where the chapel was. It turned there and then drove back into town. Rosie waited at the side of the road to catch the bus on its return journey. She could not wait to tell Ellie the news that Jim O'Loan had asked her out. Ellie would be pea green with envy.

Just then a car pulled up alongside Rosie and she saw Sean O'Loan reach over and wind down the passenger side window.

"Are you going into town Rosie?" he enquired. She answered that she was, but when he offered her a lift Rosie refused saying that she was OK getting the bus. Sean O'Loan smiled at her and pointed out that it was going to rain and she might as well have a lift as he was going that way. Rosie hesitated. Sean O'Loan might one day be her brother-in-law and she did not want to offend him anymore than was necessary, even if he had made fun of her.

"OK, thanks!" she said, and jumped into the car beside him.

"Where abouts are you going Rosie?" Sean asked.

"I'm going to Ellie's house . . . but you can just drop me anywhere in town and I can walk down there," she replied, trying to sound polite but casual. Sean didn't know who Ellie was but he figured she lived somewhere in Tullymore.

"I'll drop you right to her door Rosie. It'll save you getting wet," he said, managing to make Rosie feel like a small child. It was starting to rain and Rosie had no coat or umbrella with her. She did not fancy getting soaked and it was a good fifteen minute walk from the bus stop to Ellie's house. Anyway Sean had not *offered* so much as made a statement of fact. He would drop her to Ellie's door whether she protested or not.

As they drove along, Rosie became increasingly uncomfortable sitting beside this strange, silent man. He was nowhere near as handsome as his younger brother but, like Jim, he had incredibly long eyelashes and when he looked at her she felt as if he could see inside her. While Jim wore a frank and open expression, Sean's eyes betrayed an inner pain and suspicion. *Probably he's just jealous* thought Rosie. After all Sean's younger brothers were all better looking and, from what Rosie could tell, smarter and wittier. Indeed Sean was not one for idle chit chat; Rosie's attempts at conversation were met by monosyllabic responses and the odd smart comment. Having offered her a lift to town; he did not seem to feel the need to talk to her. *Two can play at that game* thought Rosie as she promptly lapsed into silence. It did not last long. Rosie was incapable of not speaking when she was nervous and she was very nervous now. She wondered if Jim had confided in his elder brother about his meeting with her that morning. She decided to bring up his name so that she might assess Sean's reaction.

"I met Jim this morning down by the Wee Lough" she said, and waited for a response. "Oh" said Sean, "that must have been nice for you". Rosie snorted and turned her face towards the passenger window. Sean decided to indulge her need to talk.

"Did he tell you he's going to America?" he said.

Rosie quickly turned round again and, unable to hide her concern, asked Sean when and why Jim was going away.

"He's looking to work over there for a while, maybe emigrate if he likes it."

Rosie was stunned at this reply.

"But what about his work here and . . . . everything?" she stammered, trying to sound unconcerned.

"Well, there *are* five of us you know Rosie, and I'm sure we can manage to run the business without Jim . . . for a while at least" replied Sean. Rosie was devastated.

"Are you all right Rosie?" enquired Sean after some moments during which Rosie had maintained a stunned silence.

"Yeah, sure" she said but there were tears in her eyes. Sean noticed them and looked concerned. He knew that Rosie had a crush on Jim but surely she could not have any hold over him? It was Sean's turn to be worried.

The whole family were behind Jim's decision to go to the States. Sean in particular wanted his brother to travel and see the world before settling down. Sean had been working in the family business since he was fourteen; but he had worked and travelled abroad when he was twenty-one, spending six months in Australia, six months in Canada and another six months travelling round the States. He had also been to Figi, New Zealand, Hawaii and Mexico, and had travelled extensively in Europe. He did not want his younger brother to lose out. A girl like Rosie could certainly mess things up for Jim.

Sean stopped the car. They had arrived at Ellie's house. Rosie thanked him for the lift and was about to get out of the car when Sean spoke,
"Rosie wait!" He paused for a moment, as if struggling to find the right thing to say.
"I know you like Jim, but he really wants to go to New York. We have family over there that can get him started. It would be a whole new life for him away from this shithole country." She knew that he spoke sincerely, but Rosie was not in the mood to hear what Sean had to say. She wanted to confront Jim. She longed to ask him if he was really going away and if he ever intended coming back, but she knew she had no right to ask him. He had kissed her for the first time today after a chance encounter which he had not planned. It might have meant nothing to him. Yet she was

sure that it had been the start of something. She turned to Sean and stated as nonchalantly as she could,

"Oh I don't mind him going. In fact I'm glad for him. I hope he has a great time . . . . tell him I said *bon voyage*! . . . in case I don't see him again." She jumped out of the car, banged the car door and ran up the driveway to Ellie's house. Before she rang the bell, she turned and waved to Sean with a big smile on her face and shouted,

"Thanks again for the lift."

Before he drove off, Sean saw Ellie open the door and admit Rosie to the house. He felt bad. Sean knew that Rosie was upset and he felt responsible.

Silly wee girl he thought to himself. It's not like she was Jim's girlfriend. Half the females in the country would be crying their eyes out when they heard of Jim's departure. There was, however, something different about Rosie. She had a big heart and Sean believed that she would feel the loss deeply. Perhaps he should have been more sensitive. It was not in Sean's nature though to be soft. He had grown up looking out for his younger brothers. He was worried in particular about Jim. Tensions were running high in the country. Although the yearly death toll was not what it had been in the 70s, the commencement of an investigation into an alleged *Shoot to Kill* policy within the RUC had strengthened Republican sentiments within the area. Sean was worried about the active recruitment of young men into the IRA. The older boys in his family were more settled. They had long-term girlfriends and wives to think about and to keep them grounded: Jim was young, headstrong and passionate.

Jim had also lost a close friend two years previously in a shooting incident. Mark O'Loan was a full cousin of Jim's. His family lived near the chapel at Tullycross. He and Jim were the same age and had been friends since they were babies. Mark had been out walking with his dogs and had stepped behind the wall of an old hay shed to relieve himself. When he emerged from the behind the wall, he was shot on sight without warning. Despite a witness testimony to this effect, Mark's death was recorded as accidental. RUC Special Branch had apparently been watching the house and surrounding buildings for some time, suspecting the place of being used to store arms and explosives for the IRA. Mark had inadvertently stumbled into the middle of a top secret surveillance operation. His death had been devastating for his family, and Jim had felt his loss deeply. It had triggered in him a growing hatred for the RUC and the British Army which had previously existed in embryonic stage only.

Whenever he was stopped by the British soldiers or the RUC, Jim could not help but be *difficult*. He was always asked to get out of the car, which was usually searched from bonnet to boot. He would taunt the soldiers or the police by replying to their questions in Gaelic. He made fun of their accents and mimicked their mannerisms. Sean had warned him time and again to *wind his neck in* whenever he was dealing with the authorities. His warnings fell on deaf ears. Sean was convinced it was only a matter to time before Jim got himself into a situation that he would not be able to get out of. He already had a reputation for being a rebel with a cause. Jim, like the rest of his generation, had never known anything other than *trouble* in Northern Ireland. His grief over the loss of his friend made him vulnerable. He could be easily manipulated by rhetoric and twisted by bitterness. Sean wanted him to get away from Northern Ireland, at least until he was mature enough to be able to remove him self from any possible involvement with the paramilitaries.

For Sean it was different. He had learned at a young age how to protect himself from undesirables. He had spent a week in Castlereagh Holding Centre in 1978 where he had been interrogated on a daily basis. While any physical damage had long since healed, Sean had spoken to no one about the mental torture, sleep deprivation and intimidation he had been subjected to while being *held*. He had been travelling to work one day when the van he was driving had been hijacked. Three men in masks ordered him at gunpoint to get into the back of the van and be quiet until told otherwise. He did not need to be told twice. Unfortunately for the hijackers, the van was stopped at a routine army road block not far from the hijacking. After a brief attempt to shoot their way out, the terrorists had surrendered. Sean was found in the back of the van by the soldiers and escorted to Castlereagh. Despite recovering his identification from the van, which confirmed who he was, Sean was put in a cell with the men who had hijacked him. Needless to say he was encouraged to keep his 'fuckin' mouth shut'. After a week in Castlereagh, Sean was transferred to Crumlin Road Jail where he remained on remand for a further three weeks. He was ultimately released on bail, but had to face a lengthy and expensive trial, which nearly bankrupt the family business. In the end, a singularly sensible judge decided that there was no case against him. The whole experience left Sean cynical about life and reticent about divulging information of any sort, in particular personal information, to anyone.

Sean thought about Rosie as he drove away. She was very pretty and not without her charms, but she was young and, in his opinion, she was a bit *light*. If Jim started seeing her now he might change his mind about going to the States. Sean decided to talk to Jim about her when he got home. He was not about to have his plans for Jim messed up by a wee girl like Rosie Maguire.

Meanwhile, Ellie and Rosie were sitting in the *good room* in Ellie's house. Ellie's younger siblings were not allowed in, and her elder brothers were not at home. The girls had peace to talk. Rosie had been planning what to tell Ellie since her encounter with Jim that morning but, in light of what Sean had just told her, she now did not know where to start. Ellie prompted her to start *at the beginning*. Rosie talked in great detail about the walk on the hill, the meeting with Jim, falling in the mud, Jim lifting her over the hedge, and last of all, the kiss. Ellie was enthralled.

"Did he ask to see you again?" she enquired as soon as Rosie had stopped talking.

"Yes" replied Rosie, "he said he'd call me during the week."

"Oh, you lucky bitch!" squealed Ellie. She was genuinely delighted for her friend and considered her to be extremely fortunate that she had finally managed to attract the attention of the much sought after Jim O'Loan. Rosie then adopted a look of complete misery and dejection.

"What's the matter Rosie?" her friend asked.

Rosie responded in characteristically dramatic style,

"Well, I was waiting on the bus to come into town and Sean O'Loan, Jim's creepy brother, pulled up and asked if I wanted a lift, so he ended up dropping me down to your house . . ."

"I wondered who's the car was" Ellie interjected,

"Well guess what he's after telling me . . . ." Rosie said, pausing for maximum dramatic effect,

"What? . . . What?" Ellie urged,

". . . only that Jim is emigrating to America and . . . I'll . . . never see him again!" Rosie burst into tears. Ellie immediately put her arm around Rosie's shoulder and attempted to comfort her.

"Here, have a smoke" she said. Rosie immediately responded to the offer in the affirmative. She hadn't had a cigarette since the night before and, all heartbreak aside, she was *choking* for one. Neither Ellie nor Rosie were allowed to smoke but, given that Ellie's mother and brothers were out of the house, and such a crisis warranted it, the girls lit up in the *good room* and shared a cigarette. All reverence was afforded the ritual and neither spoke until the cigarette was finished down to the last draw. Ellie then asked her friend when Jim was going to America. Rosie realised then that she did not actually know. *Perhaps he was just thinking about it. Perhaps he wouldn't go now that they were an item. Perhaps she was crying for nothing.* She looked at Ellie and said,

"I don't know."

"Well you'll have to find out. After all, there's many a slip twixt the cup and the lip." Rosie looked at Ellie with unveiled admiration.

"You know, you're right. I bet Sean O'Loan was just winding me up. He's a real wind up merchant you know."

"Yeah" agreed Ellie, who did not actually know Sean at all, "I bet that's what it is. I mean, what would Jim be asking you out for if he's going to America?"

"That's right. I'll just ask Jim when he phones me. Oh, Ellie, what if he doesn't phone me at all?" Fresh anxiety and drama was thus introduced to the conversation and Ellie was again called upon to reassure her friend.

"Why would he say he'd phone you and then not?" Ellie asked, trying to sound convincing. Rosie looked at her and realised that Ellie was not that sure that the promised phone call would happen.

"Because he's a fella, Ellie" she wailed with renewed desperation.

"Well there's no point getting your knickers in a twist! You'll just have to wait and see" Ellie stated, matter-of-factly.

Frankly, Ellie was becoming a bit frustrated with Rosie's obsession about Jim O'Loan. Both girls had fancied him from the age of fourteen when they had first seen him at the disco in the parochial hall at Tullycross. Ellie however, being more pragmatic than Rosie, had not allowed her attraction to Jim to become exclusive. She had fancied other boys since then and the current love interest in her own life was, in her opinion, a lot more accessible than *Adonis* himself, Jim O'Loan. Ellie believed that the fun in any romance was the chase; once a man showed any interest in her whatsoever Ellie tended to lose interest herself. Now that Rosie had managed to attract Jim, why on earth was she so concerned about what happened next? So what if he went to America? Plenty more fish in the sea reasoned Ellie. She did not share her feelings with her friend as she knew the depth of Rosie's feelings for Jim, but seriously she thought; get over your self Rosie!

The girls decided to go for a walk to the shop to buy cigarettes. Rosie hadn't enough money but, between the pair of them, they could afford ten *Regal Kingsize*. They set off up the road which led to the shop and then to the graveyard. The hedge surrounding the graveyard bordered the playing fields of the local Catholic high school, St Catherine's, which both girls attended. After purchasing their cigarettes Ellie suggested they visit the graveyard. As they wandered around the graves the girls commented on the ages of the residents.

"Here's a wee lad who died when he was only twelve" pointed out Rosie, as she stopped to read the inscription on one of the stones, "when I was wee I wanted to die when I was twelve" she continued.

"What?" said Ellie, in disbelief. "Why on God's earth would you *want* to die when you're only twelve?"

"Well, when I was *actually* twelve I didn't want to die. When I was twelve I wanted to die when I was twenty-four, like James Dean. But when I was little, about six or seven, I thought twelve was ancient . . . . and St Agnes died when she was twelve. She was a virgin martyr".

"Well at least *you* don't have to worry about dying a virgin Rosie" sniggered Ellie. "You're awful" retorted Rosie, hitting her friend on the arm before continuing, "anyway, now that I am seventeen I don't think I want to die when I'm twenty-four any more either: maybe thirty-six, like Marilyn Monroe."

Ellie looked at Rosie with mock horror.

"You are such a moron Rosie" she stated, laughing, "you'll probably die old and fat lying on your ass in bed!" Rosie started to get angry but then burst out laughing too.

"I suppose I am a bit morbid on it, but you were the one who wanted to walk around the graveyard."

"I know" said Ellie, "I thought it would make you shut up for a while!"

"Bitch!" cried Rosie, again laughing.

The girls sat down by one of the graves to have a smoke. This time they had one each. At least there was very little chance of anyone seeing them smoke when they were in the graveyard. Ellie was terrified that one of her elder brothers would catch her and tell her mother. Rosie never thought about getting caught. Her family were miles away in Tullybeg and she assumed there was *zero* chance of anyone she knew seeing her here. Unknown to herself and Ellie the head mistress of the school, Sr Mary Terese, was at that moment strolling in the graveyard herself and had spotted the girls from quite a distance. She walked silently towards them and was now within speaking distance of where they sat.

"Rosie Maguire" she began, as she approached the girls, "are you sitting on a grave AND smoking a cigarette? Have you no respect?" Rosie jumped up immediately and dropped the precious weed to the ground. Ellie had put her cigarette out before Sr Mary Terese had spoken and the elderly nun had not actually seen her smoking. As usual Rosie's automatic response was to lie,

"No sister" she said.

"Then what's that lying there?" enquired the nun, pointing to the, still smouldering, fag end.

"It's not mine, Sister, or Ellie's either." Rosie replied. "There were big lads here a minute ago and they must have left it there".

The older woman turned to Ellie and asked her out right, "Were you smoking Ellie?"

"Yes sister, I was" replied Ellie, looking the nun straight in the eye. "I'm sorry Sister, the cigarette is mine. Rosie was just trying to cover for me." Rosie squirmed and was unable to look up from the ground. St Mary Terese was impressed with Ellie.

"At least you are honest Miss McKeown" she said, before turning to Rosie and continuing, "you, however, are a liar Rosie Maguire. You will end up in a bad state if you continue to lie and to disrespect yourself and other people. Now, both of you leave this sacred place before you offend anyone else!"

Sr Mary Terese smiled to herself as the two girls scurried off in the direction of the main road. She could still smell the smoke in the air. She inhaled deeply. It reminded her of a time when she too had enjoyed a cigarette. That was, however, many years ago and she was a different person now.

Chapter Three

"Walk me up to the bus Ellie" said Rosie. They were in Ellie's room listening to records. *Ruby Tuesday* was just finishing. Ellie was enjoying listening to her brother's Rolling Stones LP. She only got to hear it when he was out of the house and she wanted to listen to the rest of the album.

"No way, Rosie, then I have to walk down town by myself."

"So, what are you afraid of?" Rosie snapped. "After all I came the whole way into town to see you. The least you could do is walk me to the bus."

"OK, OK!" sighed Ellie . . . "but I'm only going half way."

"All right" agreed Rosie.

They left the house in good spirits. The sun had come out and it was a pleasant, warm afternoon.

"I wonder what Jim's doing now" Rosie mused, as they strolled along.

"Boring!" Ellie replied, but seeing Rosie's face cloud over, she continued,

"He's probably lying on his bed thinking sexy thoughts about you Rosie."

"Do you really think so?" Rosie asked, turning to her friend and catching the smile on Ellie's face,

"Ha Ha! Ellie, you just think it's all a big joke that I'm in love and it's breaking my heart that he's leaving me."

"No, Rosie, I don't, but I mean, let's face it. You're seventeen. So what if he goes to America. We'll be going to Queen's next year and sharing a flat and having fun ourselves, like we planned! . . . . remember?"

"I suppose so . . . . but I'll really die if he goes away."

"You will not" replied Ellie, in her most assertive voice. "you'll probably just get depressed and fat, and he'll be glad he left you!"

"I will not," retorted Rosie, "I'll pine for him . . . and you always lose weight when you pine."

"Rosie, the day you stop eating is the day I grow a willie and call myself Edward!" laughed Ellie. Rosie could not help but laugh too. The idea of Ellie turning into a man was ridiculous. She was without doubt the most *girlie* girl that Rosie had ever known. Ellie was always well dressed, wore make up and perfume at all times, and had perfectly manicured nails. She was not a classic beauty but she had an innate sexiness that either terrified or attracted the opposite sex in equal quantities.

"You, Miss Ellie, are no lady" said Rosie in her best Southern Belle accent.

"And you, Miss Rosie, are an asshole!" replied Ellie in similar fashion. The two girls laughed together, attracting the attention of more than one passer by. They had reached the large chapel near the centre of town when Ellie, remembering herself, said,

"Hey, I walked way more than half way so you're on your own."

"OK" said Rosie, "I'll see you later." They said their good byes and Rosie promised to phone her friend that night.

Rosie hurried onwards realising that she had only a few minutes to reach the bus stop before the last bus home departed. She started to run and, without looking, attempted to cross the road at the same time. Unnoticed by Rosie, a car was about to pull up alongside the pavement as she stepped out onto the road. Rosie froze as she heard the screech of brakes and felt a thud against her left leg. She crumpled up and hit the ground. Before she could gather herself Rosie heard the voice of a man shouting her name. She then felt two hands grab her face while two eyes looked searchingly into her own. Although conscious, Rosie was in shock, and there was a sharp pain shooting up and down her leg. She recognised the face of Sean O'Loan. Looking up she said,

"I'm sorry" as she attempted to stand. Sean told her not to move and proceeded to feel her legs and arms all over in an attempt to check if anything was broken. Sean had not been driving fast. In fact, he had slowed almost to a standstill intending to pull up beside Rosie and offer her a lift. He could not believe it when she ran out in front of his car. He was deeply shocked and could barely stop himself shaking as Rosie assured him she was fine and again attempted again to stand up. This time Sean helped her to her feet. She winced as she tried to put her left leg to the ground. Without hesitating Sean swept her into his arms and carried her to the car where he placed her in the back seat.

"I'm taking you to the hospital Rosie" he said.

"Wise up Sean! I'm alright," argued Rosie, who was still worrying about missing the bus home.

"You need to get that leg seen to Rosie"

"But I'll miss my tea" continued Rosie, who could think of nothing other than the trouble she'd be in if the bus arrived home without her.

"Rosie, you've had an accident and you need to go to the hospital, OK!" It was not a request. Sean was taking her to the hospital.

"OK, OK" she muttered.

As it was Sunday, there were only a few people about when Rosie collided with Sean's car. Sean assured those passers-by who had gathered at the scene that it would be quicker if he took Rosie to hospital rather than wait for an ambulance. One or two of the older people nodded in agreement and, having gained their consent to his plan of action, Sean drove Rosie to the hospital. The hospital was some four miles from town. Sean drove as fast as experience and fear would allow him. He did not want to get stopped by the police, but he was worried in case Rosie had sustained any sort of head injury or internal damage.

"How are you feeling Rosie?" he asked, looking into the rear view mirror and attempting to see her facial expression.

"I'm a bit hungry" she replied.

"I mean your leg, Rosie, is it sore?" Sean said irritably.

"I'm sure I'll live" Rosie replied, imitating the response Sean had given her that morning when she had enquired after his mother. Sean's face clouded over and he felt something akin to remorse for having teased her. He continued to look at her frequently in the rear view mirror as they drove along in silence. She had a pretty face. She looked attractive now when she wasn't talking. *Silly wee girl* Sean thought, for the second time that day. This time though he could not help but smile at her reflection. She did not notice.

They arrived at the hospital and Sean pulled up outside the emergency room.

"Sean, you're not allowed to park here" Rosie pointed out, reading a large sign, "it's for emergencies only."

"You *are* an emergency Rosie" Sean sighed, jumping out of the car and running to get a wheel chair from the porter's office.

"Oh" she said, "right enough!"

Rosie was suddenly aware of the dramatic nature of her predicament. *What if they keep me in? I wonder will Jim come and visit me?* She thought, beginning to realise the full potential of her situation. At the same time she became aware of the searing pain in her leg. Her back and arms were also beginning to ache and Rosie suddenly felt quite queasy. She felt as if she was going to be sick but, seeing Sean approach with a wheel chair, she choked down the vomit and tried to get out of the car. As she put her foot to the ground she screamed in pain and promptly threw up all over the side of Sean's car. Sean panicked. He called to the porter who had been following him. The porter grabbed Rosie before she fell to the ground and managed to get her seated while Sean held the chair in place.

"You better move the car," said the porter, "I'll take her inside".

Sean slammed the back door of the car shut, ignoring the vomit. He then drove the car into the car park and hastened back to the emergency room. Rosie was talking to the triage nurse about her brother.

"Yeah, I'm in the same class as your Mark. He's a real laugh. Tell him I said hello."

"I will" replied the nurse, who recognised Rosie as soon as she was wheeled into the emergency room.

"So what happened to you Rosie?" the nurse asked. Rosie noticed Sean standing at the door,

"HE ran over me" she laughed, pointing to Sean.

"Now why would you want to do that?" the nurse asked, looking at Sean.

"You obviously don't know Rosie that well" replied Sean, raising his eyebrows and smiling knowingly at the nurse, who happened to be very attractive. She laughed. Rosie sniffed in disgust. She did not like the idea of Sean flirting with another woman at her expense.

"Is she going to be all right?" asked Sean, ignoring Rosie and talking directly to the nurse.

"Oh, she'll need an X-ray, and she'll have to see the doctor but I think she'll be OK." "Will I have to stay in the hospital tonight?" asked Rosie, who was still hoping that Jim would visit her.

"It depends on what the doctor says, but I don't think so" replied the nurse.

"Oh!" Rosie said, sounding quite disappointed.

"I thought you wanted to get home to your tea, Rosie" said Sean. The thought of food brought Rosie back down to earth. She looked at the nurse and asked:

"How long do you think it will be before I'm seen by the doctor? I'm really starving you know, I haven't eaten since two o'clock". It was now quarter past six. Sean saw the panic in Rosie's face.

"You know Rosie you won't starve, just because you miss one meal" he said. Rosie was not reassured.

"Who said I'd have to miss my tea . . . . mummy better keep me some. Sean will you ring my house and tell them what's happened. And tell them to keep my tea for me till I get home."

"I could ask them to bring it here to the hospital for you Rosie" said Sean. Rosie was giving serious consideration to this suggestion when she noticed the expression on Sean's face. Before she could say anything the nurse pointed out that she better not eat anything until after she'd seen the doctor, 'just in case'. Rosie then began to really panic,

"What do mean, will I need an operation? I'm not good with needles you know!"

"We could get them to examine your head Rosie while you're here!" said Sean. Rosie glared at him.

"You obviously need your eyes tested to," he continued, "the way you walked out in front of my car it's a wonder you're not dead."

"You needn't blame me 'cause you're a crappy driver" snapped Rosie. The pain in her leg, the shock of the fall and the recent vomiting incident was beginning to take its toll on her. Rosie suddenly turned very pale and seemed to slump in the chair. Sean was instantly at her side and called for the nurse, who had momentarily turned her back on Rosie to check some files sitting on her desk. She now looked quite concerned and told Sean to wait with Rosie while she called the doctor. Rosie had fainted. When she came round, only seconds later, Sean was kneeling beside her and holding her hand. She winced as she opened her eyes.

"Are you all right Rosie?" Sean spoke tenderly. He was genuinely concerned.

"Told you I needed food" muttered Rosie, "I'm collapsing here from starvation!"

Sean could not help but smile despite the anxiety he felt.

"You gave me a fright there Rosie."

"Serves you right for making fun of me" she replied. She was feeling better and the colour had returned to her face. A doctor entered the room and, noticing that Rosie was somewhat recovered, asked her how she felt.

"I'm fine" she said, "but I'd like to go home now and lie down. I feel like I could sleep forever."

"I think we better keep you in for observation tonight, Miss Maguire", said the Doctor.

"Will I be allowed to eat anything?" asked Rosie.

"Off course" said the doctor, I think you've just had a bad shock and I need to make sure that you have no internal injuries."

"You won't be examining her head then doctor" said Sean. The doctor was not quite sure what Sean meant at first, but seeing the look on his face he smiled and said,

"I don't think we need to do that just yet."

Later that evening, Rosie was sitting up in the hospital bed munching grapes which her mother had brought for her. The whole family had come to see her. They had just left and Rosie was feeling quite pleased with herself. *I could get used to this* she mused as she flicked through the magazine Anne had given her. She had taken strong pain killers and was feeling quite relaxed. Sean had insisted on waiting with her until her parents had arrived. He had phoned them to let them know what had happened. Mrs Maguire was upset at first but, after hearing that Rosie was not seriously hurt, she calmed down and reassured Sean that it was not his fault. Mrs Maguire further reassured Sean by telling him that Rosie had always been a jaywalker and if it hadn't been for divine intervention she would have been killed on many a previous occasion. She also told Sean that, if Rosie was going to get herself knocked down *wasn't it as well that it was by someone she knew and not a complete stranger who might have left her lying there.* Sean was strangely comforted by Mrs Maguire's words. He teased Rosie about what her mother had said. Rosie refused to rise to the ribbing, stating flatly that it was not her fault that Sean 'can't drive for shit.'

They spent almost an hour in similar banter before the Maguire clan had arrived en *masse.* Sean was actually disappointed when he saw Rosie's family enter the ward. He was enjoying the chat with Rosie and found himself not wanting to leave. He stopped briefly to apologise to Mr and Mrs Maguire again for knocking down their daughter. Having been advised not to worry himself about it, Sean said goodbye to the family and left. He smiled to himself, as he walked towards the car park, remembering Rosie's embarrassment as she apologised for puking on his car. He felt confused. His rational thought advised him that Rosie Maguire was a twit of the highest order. She was uncouth, scruffy and foul mouthed. Sean was used to dating sophisticated, independent women of his own age. Experience taught him that women either expected to be cajoled like children, pampered like pets or conquered like wild animals. Rosie did not fit into any of these categories. She was as readable as an open book. She was unassuming and unaffected yet she was definitely *full of mad dog shit.* Sean decided Rosie Maguire was the type of girl best avoided and he determined then that that's what he would do.

When Sean arrived home, Mrs O'Loan was just wetting a pot of tea. She placed the tea pot on the Aga stove and it began to simmer instantly. She then asked Sean what had kept him so long in town. Sean told his mother about the accident. As he spoke he poured a cup of tea for himself and his mother. While they were chatting, Jim O'Loan entered the kitchen. He had just showered and changed his clothes. His hair was still damp; he ran a comb through it as his mother and Sean continued talking. He heard all about the accident, but said nothing. Grabbing his car keys from the table, he told his mother he was going out for a while. Before either Sean or Mrs O'Loan, could speak, Jim was in his car driving towards the hospital.

When he heard Sean mention Rosie as being the girl he had knocked down, Jim was shocked to the core. He was still high from his encounter with Rosie by the Wee Lough that morning. He had spent the day thinking about her. Jim was definitely attracted to Rosie, but he could not help wondering if he was wise getting involved with anyone when his plan was to go to the States. He decided that it would be better not to see Rosie again. Jim hoped to be in New York by the end of August and was working hard to save the money he would need to get himself set up. He reasoned that he did not have the time to have a girlfriend and, after all, it would not be fair on Rosie to go out with her now. As he drove towards the hospital Jim was not thinking about New York. He was thinking about what might have happened to Rosie. He could not deny the anxiety and concern he felt when he thought about her being in any sort of pain.

When he reached the ward where Rosie was staying, the staff would not allow him to enter as visiting time was over. Jim pleaded with the Sister in charge saying that he had only found out about the accident and that he was Rosie's boyfriend. The Sister was not an unfeeling woman; she couldn't help but melt under the charm of such an exceptionally good looking lad as Jim. She allowed him five minutes 'and no more mind!' The grateful smile Jim flashed her was reward enough. Sister's heart melted and she giggled like a school girl as she waddled up the corridor remembering past conquests of her own.

Jim now took time to feel nervous about meeting Rosie again. When he saw her though, she smiled so sweetly and looked so eager to see him that all anxiety left him and he sauntered over to her as if she was his own. He sat down beside her bed and immediately asked how she felt.

"I'm fine . . . now" replied Rosie. She had been in the depths of despair moments before when she had given up hope that Jim would visit her. Now she felt elated and would gladly have left the hospital bed and thrown her arms round his neck if she had not been acutely aware of her state of undress. Mrs Maguire had brought Rosie one of her own nightdresses which, though new, was old fashioned with a high collar and volumes of unnecessary material. Rosie thought it looked like a tent.

"Our Sean said that you hurt your leg. It's not broken or anything?" asked Jim.

"No, no, it's only a scratch. I just got a bit of a shock, that's all."

"Our Sean should be more careful when he's driving" muttered Jim.

"Ach, it wasn't his fault really" said Rosie, "I was running for the bus and I wasn't looking where I was going."

"Well, I suppose it could have been worse" reflected Jim, "you could have been killed and then where would I be?"

Rosie's face flushed with pleasure at his words, but she made an attempt to sound careless in her reply,

"Oh, I dare say you would pick someone else out of the gutters to replace me!" Jim laughed,

"Ah but Rosie I don't know anyone else that looks as well covered in muck as you do. In fact, I think the colour of muck suits you down to the ground."

"I promise to wear it always" she said. Jim looked at her as she laughed. Without thinking, he bent over and kissed her before she could speak again.

"I'm glad you're alright Rosie," he said, as he stood up to leave. "I better go now. The nurse said I was only to stay a minute." Rosie looked disappointed.

"Well I should be home tomorrow anyway" she said, prompting Jim to reply,

"I'll call you then."

"Good!" said Rosie, forgetting herself. "I mean, OK, then!" Jim said goodbye and walked out of the ward. Rosie looked around to see if any of the other patients had noticed how handsome he was. She was rewarded with a jealous stare from a girl in the bed opposite hers. Rosie's heart swelled with pride and joy.

Chapter Four

Three days later Rosie awoke in her own bed feeling deflated. She had been discharged from hospital on Monday afternoon and spent the evening and the following day waiting for the phone to ring. Every time it did, she jumped to answer it; on each occasion she was sorely disappointed when it wasn't Jim. She was irritated beyond belief whenever anyone else in the house spent more than a minute talking on the phone. *What if Jim was trying to get through to her and the line was engaged?* Kate pointed out that if Jim O'Loan was keen on her he would keep trying. Rosie was not so sure. By Wednesday morning she was convinced that Jim was not interested in her, and she was doomed to spend eternity wondering the earth with a broken heart like Catherine Earnshaw. It was only the quest for breakfast that motivated Rosie to rise. If she had not been hungry she would probably have spent several more hours in bed indulging her bleakest thoughts and generally feeling sorry for herself. As it was, hunger drove her to the kitchen where she helped herself to *Weetabix,* while waiting for her toast to pop up. *Weetabix* provided instant gratification: toast took 'absolutely ages'.

When the toast was *finally* ready, Rosie spread it with butter and her mother's home-made strawberry jam. The strawberries had ripened early that year; Mrs Maguire had already managed to make several pots of jam. Rosie had personally consumed almost two of them in a week. Rosie considered home-made strawberry jam to be, without a doubt, the best food in the entire world and she could not resist it. She felt instantly happier while she munched her toast and, momentarily at least, all thoughts of Jim O'Loan were expelled to her unconscious mind. The flavour of sweetened strawberries consumed her being and Rosie was in heaven as she savoured each mouthful. As she often did, Rosie hummed while she ate. It was not something she was conscious of doing, being an automatic response to the inner joy she experienced when she was eating. "Yummmm!" she sighed, as she finished that last bite, washing it down with a mouthful of tea.

"Are you talking to your toast Rosie?" asked Orlagh, who had just come into the kitchen. "Yes, I am. It makes more sense than anyone in *this* house!" replied Rosie, smiling at her sister and wondering if she should have another slice. Orlagh sniggered,

"You're mad Rosie."

"I am that, Orlagh, but as granny would say, I'm doing no one any harm! Anyway, what are you at today?" Rosie was displaying an uncommon interest in her youngest sister, which unnerved Orlagh. She was instantly suspicious,

"Nothing" she replied.

"Good, well, you can do the dishes" laughed Rosie, as she sauntered out of the kitchen leaving her plate and cup in the sink along with the pile of other breakfast things.

"That's not fair!" wailed Orlagh after her, "I've to do everything!" Her cries fell on deaf ears; Rosie was already in the bath room stripping off in preparation for her shower.

Rosie had arranged to meet Ellie in town. After spending more time than usual at her toilette, she begged the price of the bus fare from her mother and ran to catch the half past twelve bus. When the bus arrived in town, Ellie was waiting at the bus stop as planned. The girls immediately headed to their favourite pub. The pub overlooked the main street and the large protestant church in the centre of town. While the entrance was on the street, the bar itself was on the second floor with a steep stair case leading up to it. The girls took their usual seat at the window which allowed them to look down on the passers by. After purchasing two glasses of cider Ellie and Rosie pooled their cigarettes and found that they had six in total. Three cigarettes each and one glass of cider allowed them the luxury of sitting for at least an hour in the pub without feeling the need to buy another drink. Rosie immediately brought up the topic of Jim O'Loan. Ellie was in good form and decided to listen to her friend, at least for a while. Rosie shared her deepest concerns about her relationship with Jim, and after spending twenty minutes bewailing the fact that he had not phoned her she finally decided to allow Ellie the opportunity to respond.

Ellie had long since ceased paying attention to what Rosie was saying. She was thinking about what to wear on Saturday night. The girls went to a disco on the outskirts of town every weekend without fail. What to wear was always a big discussion point. Ellie always gave the subject much consideration and a lot of forethought. Rosie, as usual, left everything to the last minute and generally ended up borrowing clothes from her unfortunate sisters or from Ellie.

"I think I'll wear my hippy skirt and top on Saturday night," said Ellie in response to Rosie's request for her opinion on the subject of Jim O'Loan's failure to phone.

"What?" demanded Rosie, "were you not listening to me? I was talking about my broken heart and you're just thinking about stupid clothes!"

"Yeah, yeah Rosie, what's new?" Ellie replied, looking bored. Rosie affected a look of utter dejection and sighed deeply before saying,

"I suppose I'm just a burden to you?"

"Yes, actually, you are Rosie," said Ellie, "but we all have our crosses to bear!"

"Bitch!" snapped Rosie.

"Stupid bitch" retorted Ellie. She looked at Rosie's face then and began to feel sorry for her. Rosie was, after all, *deeply in love* with Jim. Ellie decided to provide some comfort to her friend.

"I mean, the fact is that if he phones, happy days! If he doesn't phone, he's a pig and you're better of without him!" she said. Rosie pondered these words momentarily. She did not feel reassured, but she could not help smiling at Ellie's attempt to make her feel better.

"Never join the diplomatic core, Ellie, you'd cause World War III in a week!" she said. The two girls laughed and lit up a cigarette each.

"Hey, I wonder will Jim be out on Saturday night" said Rosie, suddenly feeling more positive than she had done since her breakfast. Although it was not quite the change of subject Ellie had hoped for, she could at least relate to the topic of Saturday night.

"What are you going to wear Rosie?" she asked.

"My ma made Kate a lovely dress which I was thinking of borrowing, but I don't think she'll lend it to me after the shoe incident" said Rosie, "anyway, it's too long for me and I have no shoes to wear with it. Can I wear your hippy skirt and top?"

"I just said I was going to wear that!" replied Ellie looking annoyed. "Honestly, you never listen to anything I say Rosie".

Rosie had the good grace to look sorry.

"I do listen to you Ellie," she said, before turning her head to the side and muttering, "it's not my fault if I fall asleep at the sound of you're voice." Ellie glared at her friend before reaching across the table and nipping Rosie on the arm.

"Aow! You rat bag! I was only joking!" squeaked Rosie, rubbing her wounded flesh. "Well you're the one who has been droning on about Jim O'Loan till I'm near demented and you have the audacity to imply that I am boring!" said Ellie, furiously stubbing out her cigarette in the ashtray, extinguishing all signs of life from the crumbled butt.

"Some people have no sense of humour," simpered Rosie.

Ellie gazed out of the window. She longed to leave Tullymore. "I can't wait to get out of this shit-hole," she said. "Every thing is always the same. Same people, same places, same shit, different day."

"I know" said Rosie, "as soon as I'm eighteen I'm going to New York."

"Last week it was Greece," Ellie pointed. "suddenly it's New York. I wonder why?"

Rosie looked shocked.

"I was always thinking of America" she replied. "Really! I mean it IS the land of opportunity.

"You just want to go there because Jim O'Loan is going there. You are so fickle Rosie" stated Ellie emphatically. "You wanted to go to Greece because Anne is going there. You want to go to Queens because everyone you know is going there. You want to go to Atlanta because Scarlett O'Hara lived there. You never have an original idea of your own."

"Yes, I do!" exclaimed Rosie indignantly, "my main plan is to go *anywhere* that *you* won't be!"

"Suits me!" retorted Ellie. "I'll be long gone from Tullymore before you!"

Ellie was six months older than Rosie and already had a Plan B if she failed to get the grades to go to university. She would go to England to train as a nurse. Rosie's 'plans' were not quite so tangible. She tended to live life in the express lane, racing from one platform to the next. Rosie rarely took the time to work out the finer details of any plan of action and invariably she failed to achieve even a small percentage of her *goals* in life. This was actually a blessing. If Rosie had managed to fulfil her dreams she would have soared high momentarily, like Icarus on his false wings, only to have plunged low into the chaos that inevitably followed any action of Rosie's. To coin a phrase, Rosie was a 'walking disaster'.

While Rosie and Ellie were spending the afternoon chatting in the pub, Jim O'Loan was working with his brother Sean on a building site in the town centre. Things were strained between the two men, and conversation was currently non-existent. When Jim had returned from the hospital on Sunday evening Sean had spoken to him about his relationship with Rosie. Initially Jim refused to discuss Rosie other than to accuse his brother of negligent driving for running her over.

"For fuck's sake Jim, the girl just ran out in front of the car!" Sean replied furiously. "It wasn't my fault." Jim had apologised, but he was in no mood to listen to Sean's advice on women. Sean tried to point out that it would be better all round if Jim did not see Rosie again, given that he was going to America and may not be back home for many years. Jim denied having any intentions of seeing Rosie again but felt honour bond to point out that it was his life to do with as he saw fit and Sean couldn't stop him seeing Rosie if he wanted to. Sean had then employed more tact than was his natural inclination. He told Jim that, of course, he would respect his decision either way; he just didn't want Jim to get 'tied down'. The thought of anyone tying him down incensed Jim and he was instantly determined not to see Rosie again. He did not tell Sean this, and his brother had been left wondering what Jim's intentions were with regards to Rosie. This had caused a glitch in the, otherwise excellent, relationship between the brothers.

Three days on, however, Jim's resolve was waning. He had thought about Rosie often over the past few days. He wondered what she was doing and if she was angry that he had not phoned. He felt ashamed that he had not telephoned her after he had said he would. He felt he had now lost the opportunity to ask her out casually, or even to speak to her, without some degree of discomfort. He was also angry with Sean. He was vaguely aware of having been manipulated by his elder brother but could not remember exactly what Sean had said to accomplish this goal. Jim was currently in an extremely bad mood. Sean was aware that Jim was struggling with his feelings. It was however, impossible for two men of that generation to discuss openly their feelings. Sean was forced to find an alternative method to get his relationship with Jim back on track.

"Fancy a pint" he said, as Jim was clearing up after the lunch. Jim looked at him. This was a singularly unheard of suggestion for his brother to make during the middle of a work day. Jim was gob smacked. His automatic response was in the affirmative and before long the two men were making their way on foot to the very establishment wherein sat Rosie and Ellie.

As the church clock chimed half past one, Jim and Sean bounded up the stairs into the bar and proceeded to order two pints. The bar man poured the creamy black liquid slowly into a pint glass, bantering with Sean while he did. As he waited for his drink, Jim turned and glanced casually around the room to see if he knew anyone. His eyes fell upon Rosie who was staring at him from her seat at the window. Jim was rendered speechless by the sight of her in unexpected surroundings. He turned quickly back to the bar without so much as nodding at her. Rosie's heart sank. The joy of seeing Jim was instantly replaced by despair at his obvious snub. Ellie felt for her friend and reaching over to pat Rosie on the hand she said,

"Just ignore him Rosie. He's obviously too embarrassed to speak to you."

Rosie eyes filled with tears but she rubbed them away and attempted to pull herself together.

"Sean," whispered Jim to his brother, "there's Rosie Maguire over there. I better go."

Sean had just tasted his pint and was looking forward to sitting down and relaxing.

"Fuck sake, Jim, I've just paid for two pints. I'm not going now. Just let on you didn't see her" he said irritably.

"I can't just ignore her" replied Jim. He paused momentarily before making up his mind to speak to her, "I'm going over to say hello."

"No way Jim, then we'll have to sit with them."

"So! You can talk to her mate," offered Jim, who was already preparing himself for another encounter with Rosie. Sean glanced over to the table were the girls were sitting. He eyed Ellie up and down and, though he thought she looked quite interesting, he was not inclined to talk to either of the girls. "I'm not sitting with two wee girls talking shite," he retorted, but Jim was already walking towards the girls table. Sean followed reluctantly.

"Hello Rosie," said Jim, "Ellie" he continued, nodding his head and looking at her, unable to look at Rosie, "this is my brother Sean."

"Hello Sean" said Ellie casually.

"Do you mind if we join you?" asked Jim, directing the question to Ellie.

"I don't mind Jim. What do you think Rosie?"

"It's a free country" said Rosie trying to sound nonchalant.

"Actually, it isn't Rosie!" said Sean smiling, as he sat down beside her, leaving Jim to take the seat next to Ellie. "It hasn't been a free country in about eight hundred years."

"Well YOU can sit where you want I suppose!" said Rosie, looking briefly at Sean before turning her full attention on Jim. She was annoyed that Jim had not sat beside her, but she was overjoyed that he had come over to talk to her. All previous thoughts of heart-break were forgotten. She smiled sweetly at Jim but could think of nothing sensible to say. That didn't stop her from talking.

"Are you both off work today" she queried. It was obvious from the state of their work clothes that both men had been working very hard.

"Aye, Rosie, we've just been out shopping all morning!" said Sean, laughing and winking at Ellie.

Ellie laughed too while Jim glared at his brother. Rosie was determined not to be silenced by Sean O'Loan. "Ha Ha!" she said sarcastically, "I just meant how come you're sitting in the pub on a workday?"

"We're working round the corner there and we just fancied a pint" said Jim before his brother had time to respond.

"We're just having a wee glass of cider" said Rosie, worried that Jim might think she frequently drank during the day.

"Personally I'd love to get blocked" said Ellie, "but you know what they're like. We'd be the talk of the town by the end of the day."

"Yeah," agreed Sean, "I know what you mean. You'd get your name in the *Tullymore Times*."

"Well, I suppose if they're talking about you they're leaving someone else alone," said Ellie.

They all agreed as they each took a drink from their respective glasses.

"Do you girls want another drink?" asked Jim, noticing that Ellie and Rosie had almost finished their cider. The girls looked at each recognising the dilemma they were in. They both wanted another drink but did not have enough money to return the favour. Rosie looked embarrassed and said,

"Ah no, we're grand at the moment, but thanks anyway."

"Go on and have a drink. Sure you're on your holidays" urged Jim hoping to make it up to Rosie for not having phoned her. Having refused a drink once, the girls felt that they had conducted themselves like ladies. They were then happy to accept the offer of another drink. Free cider was not to be sniffed at. Jim promptly went to the bar to get two more glasses of cider. He was feeling pleased with himself. Rosie had not ignored him. She had even spoken to him and he could not help but notice the warmth in her eyes when he had eventually looked at her. He wished that Sean and Ellie would disappear so he could be alone with her. Rosie was thinking similar thoughts. She had lapsed into a day dream when Jim had left the table and was staring into her, now empty, glass with a whimsical look on her face.

"It's OK Rosie, plenty more where that came from!" said Sean, noticing Rosie sigh deeply.

"I wasn't thinking about that" laughed Rosie. Ellie excused herself from the table at that moment to go to the toilet.

"What were you thinking about then Rosie?" asked Sean, after Ellie left. "Have you not had your lunch?"

"I'm not hungry actually!" replied Rosie, "I was just wandering what . . . . everyone . . . will be doing this time next year . . . . or ten years from now. Do you never wonder about the future?"

"Yeah, I wonder where my next pay check's coming from and my next pint. That's about it, Rosie"

Rosie laughed,

"I guess you're right. I spend too much time thinking about what's going to happen." She was smiling but she looked sad. Sean knew she was thinking about Jim going away. He spoke more softly than usual to her.

"You know Rosie, we have years and years of this shit to live. You don't have to have it all at once."

Rosie was caught off guard by Sean's change in tone.

"I'll miss him, Sean, that's all" she said. "I'm not going to try and stop him going but I'm entitled to feel sad, OK?"

"OK, Rosie. Point taken," said Sean. "Cheer up," he continued, "you've always got me!"

"I'd rather have the plague!" laughed Rosie. Sean smiled. She *was* very cute.

Jim and Ellie both rejoined the table at the same time. Rosie and Sean were now deep in conversation and began to regale the others with the story of Rosie's accident.

"Sterling Moss here," began Rosie elbowing Sean in the arm, "was so keen to give me a lift he decided to knock me down so I couldn't refuse him."

"That wasn't they way of it at all Rosie," interrupted Sean, "she saw me coming and flung herself at my car. I was trying to escape from her."

They all laughed as Rosie and Sean continued to tease each other about the accident. When they had finished their pints Sean stood up and said,

"It's time we were away Jim." Jim nodded in agreement, but he was reluctant to leave without speaking to Rosie alone.

"I'll follow you down Sean" he said, after Sean said good bye to the girls. Rosie's heart missed a beat. Jim leaned over to her and whispered in her ear,

"I really will call you tonight." He then brushed his lips against her cheek and walked out of the bar saying good bye to Ellie as he left. Ellie looked astonished. Rosie was beaming from ear to ear.

"Oh, Ellie" she sighed, pressing her hand to the cheek that Jim had just kissed, "I'm never going to wash my face again!"

"What's new!" said Ellie, and the two girls squealed with laughter.

Jim did phone Rosie that night and the following day as well. They agreed to meet on Friday night. Rosie was overcome with excitement as the time for her first date with Jim approached. She was pacing back and forth in the hall waiting for his car to pull up outside the house. It was ten minutes to eight and he was due at eight o'clock. Mrs Maguire had watched her daughter prepare for her date with more interest than usual. Normally Rosie had a shower, blew-dried her hair, begged, borrowed or stole something to wear and slapped on some foundation, mascara and lipstick. The entire operation took twenty minutes at most. On this occasion Rosie spent an hour in the bathroom, and a further hour with Kate in her bedroom trying on different outfits.

"I hope you left that room tidy Missy" said Mrs Maguire, as Rosie peered out of the window in the hall for the hundredth time.

"I did ma," Rosie lied, wandering back into the kitchen where her mother sat doing the crossword from the *Irish News*.

"Where are you going?" asked Mrs Maguire, trying not to sound too interested.

"I don't know yet" replied Rosie.

"Well don't be too late" warned her mother, "you have your work to go to tomorrow."

"I know ma. Jim has to get up early too. He's goin' fishing."

"I hope he drives carefully. Young fellas drive far too fast you know."

"Jim's a good driver so he is" said Rosie.

"According to you, Jim's good at everything" said Mrs Maguire, turning back to her cross word.

The door bell rang at that moment and Rosie ran to answer it. It was Jim. He was in smart causal attire and smelt of an aftershave that Rosie did not recognise. Her knowledge of aftershave was confined to bottles of *Old Spice* and *Brut* which were regularly purchased for her father at Christmas time and on his birthday. Jim did not smell like Rosie's father. Rosie beamed when she saw him and shouted 'cheerio' to her mother. Mrs Maguire had come into the hall to take a look at Rosie's latest find. She knew Jim O'Loan to see, and had always considered his family to be nice people. However, a mother looks at a man differently when he is dating her daughter. Mrs Maguire nodded 'hello' to Jim. Jim smiled and said 'hello' back.

"Don't be late!" Mrs Maguire reminded Rosie, as her daughter closed the door. *That fella's far too good looking to be true* thought Mrs Maguire, as she sat down at the kitchen table and resumed her crossword.

Rosie chatted nervously as Jim drove in silence towards town.

"Where do you want to go?" he said, when Rosie finally stopped talking.

"I don't mind" said Rosie, "you're the driver." Jim continued to drive for a while before turning towards the Marina. The Marina was situated in an inlet of Lough Neagh and there were many small sailing boats moored there. Jim parked the car. Rosie immediately jumped out. She loved the water and was fascinated by the sight of boats.

"I wish I owned a boat," she said. Jim had casually followed her to the end of the wooden jetty. She was examining a particularly large yacht.

"When I'm rich Rosie, I'll buy you one" said Jim. Rosie turned and looked at him.

"Sure when you're rich you'll be living in America and you'll have forgotten all about me" she said smiling. Jim looked embarrassed but he held her gaze.

"I don't think you'll be that easy to forget. You're kinda annoying, you know . . . . like a rash."

Rosie reached out to hit him but he grabbed her hand. She tried to pull away but he held her tightly. He looked down at her face. Pulling her towards him, he kissed her. Rosie immediately stopped struggling and responded warmly. She then remembered that she was angry with Jim and took a step back,

"You know you might have told me you were going away" she said petulantly. "What did ya' think I would do? Fling myself under a bus!"

"Well you did walk out in front of our Sean's car, you know. What was I to think Rosie?" Rosie couldn't help but laugh.

"You know you're not all that Jim O'Loan. I *will* survive!"

"Yeah, maybe, but you will miss me won't you?" he said, searching her face for a reaction.

"I'll cry into my pillow every night" she replied sarcastically, Scarlett O'Hara style.

"I bet ya will! You'll probably be out with someone else before the plane lands" said Jim, smiling at her.

"Maybe before it takes off!" quipped Rosie.

"You mean you won't wait for me?" asked Jim. He was only half joking. He did not like to think of Rosie with another man. He knew that he had no right to ask her to wait for him but he was not happy at the prospect of losing her either.

"Sure who knows what will happen" she said attempting to lighten the tone of the conversation. "Maybe I'll go to America too and follow you around like a lost dog. You'd be right and pissed off then, Jim O'Loan."

"I'd just let on I didn't know you!"

"I'd have to stalk you then!"

"And I'd have to have you arrested and deported back home Rosie."

"I don't want to go to America anyway" she said tossing her head like a child. "I'm going to Queen's next year with Ellie and we're going to get a flat and have wild parties!"

"I'll tell you're mother on you, Rosie Maguire, then where'll ya be?"

"I'll be an adult and no one will be able to tell me what to do."

"I don't think you should be allowed out. You'd be dangerous on your own. You can't even cross the road properly!"

"I have nine lives" laughed Rosie, "like a cat. I've only used up about six so far!"

Jim looked at her. He reached out and took her hand again as they walked along the path that led to the nearby wooded area. The place was deserted. Jim stopped suddenly and pulled Rosie towards a large tree. He pressed her against the trunk of the tree and kissed her again. Rosie was overwhelmed by his embrace. He was strong and his kisses became increasingly urgent. His hands wandered over her shoulders and down her back. She shuddered with excitement. For a brief moment Rosie attempted to think sensibly. *I really should play a little hard to get* she thought. Trembling, she pulled her face from his and attempted to look into his eyes. He was breathing heavily and his eyes flashed as he again bent to kiss her. All thoughts of resistance left her mind as she felt the warmth of his hands circling her waist and reaching under her blouse. Rosie was oblivious to everything except the passion raging through her young warm body: until she heard the sound of approaching footsteps and the laughter of children. She immediately pulled away from Jim and straightened her clothing. Jim looked bewildered at first, before he too heard the approaching voices. A man was walking with a dog and two young children. They passed by. The man said hello and smiled knowingly at Jim. Jim's face was beaming as he nodded back. Rosie could only look at the ground. She felt deeply ashamed. *So much for playing hard to get.* As if reading her thoughts Jim took her hand and said,

"Sorry, I got a bit carried away there. Are you all right?"

"Yeah, I'm grand" she replied, unable to look at him.

"Perhaps we should go for a walk" suggested Jim.

Rosie was disappointed. She wanted to be kissed again. She knew that what she felt was dangerous but her passion for Jim was such that, had he asked, she would have allowed him to take her completely in the nearby field. Rosie felt ashamed that it was Jim and not herself who had displayed restraint.

"Sacred Heart of Jesus I place all my trust in Thee" she muttered, three times under her breath. Having finished her prayer she felt strong enough to take Jim's hand as he proceeded down the path leading back to the water.

As they walked, Rosie gradually recovered her equanimity. Jim talked to her about his plans for the future. He talked openly about going to New York in August. Rosie reluctantly had to admit to herself that at least he was being honest with her. She could not fail to notice though, that his insistence on talking about his imminent departure was his way of warning her not to become too attached to him. This annoyed her; only a man would attempt to control the way he felt. Rosie was convinced that in matters of love it was impossible to dictate how one felt about another person. She did not want to think about Jim leaving. She wanted to make him love her as she loved him.

Chapter Five

It was the middle of August and Jim and Rosie had been seeing each other regularly for six weeks. They did not talk about America after their first date. Rosie had all but managed to convince herself that, when the time came, Jim would be unable to leave her. Jim had not actually told her that he loved her. Neither had he ever mentioned not going to America, but she was quietly confident that he could not go now that they were going out together. Rosie's cup of happiness was full to overflowing. She was a joy to be around and her entire family were benefiting from her happiness. Fights in the house were at an all time low and Mrs Maguire had only to ask Rosie to do a thing and it was as good as completed. The house was cleaned on a daily basis. Rosie's bedroom was tidy. She was being more than civil to the younger children and even Barney was enjoying more walks than usual.

Only Ellie remained unconvinced by the apparent change in her friend's personality. *There'll be tears before bedtime* she mused to herself one Sunday afternoon when she and Rosie were lying in the Maguire's back garden, sunning themselves. Ellie had spent the night in Rosie's house after the disco on Saturday night. Rosie had really enjoyed the night: Jim barely left her side all evening. Initially Ellie complained to Rosie about feeling like a 'gooseberry'. Rosie managed to make Ellie feel better by introducing her to some of Jim's friends who were a nice bunch of lads. They all made a fuss of Ellie and by the end of the night she had won the admiration of more than one of the group. Ellie appreciated numbers when it came to admirers. Overall it had been a wonderful evening, but Ellie was concerned that when it came to Jim O'Loan, Rosie was setting herself up for a huge fall. It was not that Ellie did not trust Jim. She was convinced that he genuinely felt a lot for Rosie. However, she could not help but worry that he was still set on going to America, regardless of his relationship with Rosie, and that she would be left to pick up the pieces when he was gone. Rosie was not going to recover from this one easily.

Rosie rolled over onto her back and sighed deeply,
"I'm too hot" she said.
"You're never done complaining Rosie" said Ellie, flicking through the pages of a magazine.
"Do you want to go for a walk?"
"Nope. I'm fine here" said Ellie. "I'm just relaxing."
"What ya reading?"
"War and Peace! What does it look like I'm reading!" said Ellie impatiently.
"Well stop reading and talk to me!" whined Rosie.
Ellie sat up and looked at Rosie,
"Do ya know, you are like a child begging for attention? I should put you in the corner. You just want to talk about Jim, don't you?"

"No, I'm just bored" replied Rosie.

"Well please be bored quietly. I'm trying to read," said Ellie, grabbing her magazine and rolling over.

Rosie attempted to sulk but could not remain quiet for more than a few seconds.

"I wonder if Jim will come to my house on Christmas day," she said out of the blue.

"Christmas!" exclaimed Ellie, "What are you talking about Christmas for? It's the middle of August."

"I know. I was just looking at that Christmas tree daddy planted last year and I was wondering if I should invite Jim to Christmas dinner in our house."

Ellie thought about what to say. She had wanted to ask Rosie about Jim's American plans for some time, but was afraid to bring the subject up for fear it would upset Rosie. Ellie decided to grab the bull by the horns.

"Rosie, I don't think you should worry about Christmas dinner just yet . . . . you might not even be going out with Jim in December. I mean, is he not heading to America soon?" said Ellie, trying to sound casual.

The words hit Rosie like a slap in the teeth. Her face grew pale and she stumbled over her reply.

"He hasn't mentioned it in weeks . . . . I just sorta thought he had forgotten about it."

"Well maybe he has . . . . but I wouldn't bet on it" said Ellie, "you know he seemed pretty set on the idea."

"Yeah, I know, but that was . . . . before."

"Before what?" asked Ellie.

"Before we . . . . you know."

Ellie looked blankly at her friend for a moment. Then she realised what Rosie was trying to tell her.

"You did it!" she squealed.

"Tell the whole world, why don't you!" snapped Rosie, looking anxiously around to see if anyone was within hearing distance.

"I can't believe you did it!" Ellie whispered, also looking around to see if anyone was listening. "What was it like?"

"I'm not telling you" said Rosie, suddenly overcome with embarrassment.

"How many times?" asked Ellie, ignoring Rosie's attempt to be discreet.

"Just once."

"When?"

"Friday night when we went for a walk, it just sort of happened."

"Oh, Rosie, you big slut!" laughed Ellie.

Rosie began to cry silently. Ellie noticed her friend's distress and instantly stopped laughing.

"I'm sorry Rosie, I was only joking" she said "you're not really a slut."

"Yes I am" wailed Rosie, "and he'll probably dump me now that he's had his way with me." She began to cry again.

Rosie was feeling extremely confused. In her head she had not intended to sleep with Jim until they were married, but the passion between them had grown to unfathomable depths. It was at the point were they could not be alone for more than a minute without wanting to rip each other's clothes off. For Rosie the passion was mixed with her naïve notions of living happily ever after and having babies. For Jim, his feelings for Rosie stopped well short of thinking about the future. He was consumed with desire for her. He thought about her all the time when he wasn't with her. When he was with her he wanted to possess her completely but, like Rosie, actually having sex was not something he had planned. He assumed that, as on previous occasions, Rosie would stop him. On Friday night things had gotten out of hand. Rosie was basking in the warmth of the setting sun, lying in the long grass on top of the hill overlooking the Wee Lough. Lying beside her Jim felt like his hero James Cagney in *White Heat*. He was *on top of the world*. Psychotic delusions aside, Jim felt as if no one could touch them. He lowered himself on top of her and gradually they peeled of any excess clothing. He was thrilled to be entirely naked beside her for the first time he dreaded her pulling away from him. Transfixed Rosie had been unable to move.

As she sat beside Ellie now, Rosie knew she would be unable to find the words to describe exactly what sex had been like. She knew that she had lost more than her virginity. She understood now what people meant when they talked about the loss of innocence. Rosie's face coloured as she recalled the first fumbled thrust Jim made inside her and her own wincing reaction. Thereafter things became a bit blurred in her memory. She could never quite recall how it had all ended only that Jim seemed to be very pleased with himself. For her part, Rosie wanted to go back to the kissing and hugging bit. That was her favourite part.

Ellie was thinking hard about what to say. She was more worried about Rosie being pregnant than her being dumped. "Rosie, did you . . . . you know, use anything?" she finally asked.
"Don't worry, I'm definitely not pregnant" replied Rosie. "My *thing* came this morning."

"Oh Thank God!" sighed Ellie. "So what you worried about?"

"It's just that I don't know what he'll expect now. You know what I mean. What if I have to do it every time we see each other?"

"And you're afraid you'll get pregnant?" asked Ellie.

"Well yes, but also . . . . he hasn't actually said he loves me yet".

"Oh, I see" said Ellie nodding her head knowingly. "Bummer!"

"Well what do you think I should do?"

Ellie thought for a moment. She was concerned about Rosie. After a while she said quietly,

"Honestly Rosie, I don't think you should do it again. What if you get pregnant and he pisses off to America and leaves you with a wee baby?"

For a moment Rosie allowed herself to picture a miniature Jim cradled in her arms, his proud father looking lovingly into her eyes. The image was obliterated by Ellie's disapproving glare.

"Don't even think about it Rosie!" snapped Ellie. "You're an idiot if you think that's the way to get a man to do anything!"

Rosie felt the wisdom of Ellie's words. She was forced to focus, albeit momentarily, on the reality of her situation. She was playing with fire and she suspected she was about to get burned badly.

"You're right, I know," she said, "but it's really hard Ellie. Sometimes when I'm with him I can hardly speak I feel so much for him. I think about him all the time. I want to be near him always. I want to touch him all the time."

"You got it bad girl" sighed Ellie shaking her head. "Maybe you should just ask him what his intentions are. See what he says."

"Nobody asks what your *intentions* are anymore Ellie" said Rosie, smiling momentarily. "Anyway, I don't want to know. What if he says he's going anyway? I think I'll die".

"You will not die, Rosie, you'll just get on with it like the rest of us."

"No Ellie" said Rosie emphatically, "I really do think I will die: maybe not my body but . . . . everything else."

"Don't say that Rosie!" Ellie was alarmed now. "He's only a fella! You'll meet plenty more."

"I know I will, Ellie, but . . . . I know that I will never love anyone again." Rosie spoke quietly with an air of fatalism which unnerved her friend.

"Rosie, you're getting all morbid now. You don't even know what he thinks. You'd be safer just asking him out right. At least then you'd know for sure" said Ellie attempting to sound positive.

"OK, I'll ask him," said Rosie, but she did not sound convinced. She remained despondent for some time.

It was not unusual for Rosie to think herself into a depressive state. One moment she might be as high as a kite, laughing and joking, the next she would be in the depths of despair. Rosie had a tendency to follow a single thought to its most sublime, ridiculous or tragic conclusion within a matter of seconds, and her moods fluctuated accordingly. Ellie was well used to her friend's mood swings. Generally she was able to tease Rosie out of her bleakest reveries, however on this occasion, Ellie remained silent for some time. She was deeply troubled by what Rosie had told her. Ellie believed that Rosie's romantic notions were idiotic but she also believed that Rosie was more than infatuated with Jim. She was not convinced that Jim felt the same way.

Elllie was not the only one who was thinking about Rosie and Jim's relationship. At that moment, Sean O'Loan was having lunch in the kitchen with his parents. Jim and the middle O'Loan brother, Brian were also there. Sean had noticed a change in Jim in the last couple of days. He appeared to be walking taller. He was more confident and had an air of self assurance about him that Sean had not noticed before. Jim was telling the family a joke and when he finished they all laughed loudly; except Sean who had not heard the punch line.

"What's wrong with you?" asked Jim, noticing that Sean had not reacted to his joke.

"Nothing, . . . just thinking that's all."

"About what?" Mrs O'Loan asked.

Sean decided to bring up the subject of America.

"About how we will manage work when Jim goes to the States."

Sean looked at Jim and waited for a response to his statement. Jim's face lost its animation immediately and he looked deeply troubled. His father, who was sitting beside him, did not notice Jim's change in expression. Laughing he said,

"Sure we'll hardly notice him gone. He never does a hands turn anyway!"

Sean and Brian both laughed too. They all knew that Jim worked harder than any of his brothers. Being the youngest, he felt the need to prove himself continually. From an early age he had competed against the elder boys for everything, including his parents' attention.

Mrs O'Loan noticed the change in Jim's face immediately. Rosie was not the only one who did not want Jim to go. She would never ask him to stay, but she knew that she would miss him terribly. Jim remained quiet. His father, noticing the lack of response to his statement said,

"Now Jim, you're not getting sensitive in your old age, are ya? I'm sure some of us will miss ya!" He smiled knowingly at his wife. There had been many discussions about the need for Jim to go away. Mrs O'Loan always agreed with her husband in the end, but in her heart she wanted him to stay. Jim stood up and lifted his half empty plate from the table. He smiled at his father and said,

"Sure maybe I'll stick around for another while." Silence descended on the room. Sean was first to speak,

"I knew that wee girl would make you change you're mind!"

"It's nothing to do with Rosie" lied Jim, "I just don't want to go right now. I was thinking of waiting till the New Year!"

"If you can't leave now Jim, you'll never go," said Sean emphatically.

"What's it got to do with you anyway Sean?" retorted Jim, becoming increasingly agitated, "I don't want to go, and you can't make me!"

Sean stood up slowly. He was incapable of expressing the myriad feelings and thoughts running through his mind. He was afraid, not for himself, but for his brother. Sean had not been afraid for himself since the day he left Castlereagh. It was as if his experience there had served to immunise him from feeling fear. Now he could not stand to feel afraid, even for another person. He felt he was losing control and this unnerved him deeply. Before he could respond Mrs O'Loan held out her hand to Jim and speaking quietly said, "Son, off course no one can *make* you go away and no one really *wants* you to leave either, but your father and me are really worried that if you stay here you'll get into . . . . bother. We just want you to be safe and away from it all . . . . for a while any way! As soon as things settle down you can come home and you know there'll always be a job for you here. We don't want you to go away forever . . . and sure if wee Rosie loves you she'll wait for you." Jim's face coloured at the mention of Rosie's name. He did not want his father or brothers to think that he couldn't go away because of a *girl*. Frankly he was having a hard time admitting this even to himself. He just knew that he did not want to face leaving Rosie just yet. All he had thought about, for the past forty-eight hours, was making love to her on the hillside beside the Wee Lough. She had mesmerised him.

Sean was not inclined to be as diplomatic as his mother. He was unreasonable in his anger. It was Rosie he was furious with. He believed she had bewitched his brother and was convinced that she would do anything to keep him in Ireland, including produce a child that would tie Jim down for eternity. Being a man of action, Sean did not say anything but determined there and then that he would speak to Rosie. Jim was in no mood to listen to him. He would go straight to the source of the problem. Sean left the house after lunch telling his mother that he was going into town. Instead of turning towards Tullymore though, he drove instead towards the Maguire house. He did not want to call for Rosie but hoped that he might just run into her somewhere. He passed by the house slowly, but there was no sign of life. He pulled in at the side of the road beyond the house and waited in his car.

At that moment, Ellie and Rosie were still lying in the back garden arguing about what to do next. Ellie wanted to remain in the garden while Rosie still wanted to go for a walk. Just then, Anne Maguire came out of the house and sat down beside the girls. She and Ellie immediately began to discuss an article in the magazine that Ellie was reading, and before long they were deep in conversation. Rosie was bored.

"I'm going for a walk" she announced. Both Anne and Ellie agreed that she should and continued to talk.

"Right I'm away then!" announced Rosie. The other girls ignored her.

Rosie wandered aimlessly towards the front gate and turned onto the road. She spotted Sean's car immediately and walking straight to it she popped her head into the open window and said,

'Hello!' Sean was startled by her abrupt salute. He had been thinking about what to say to her when she appeared.

"Hiya Rosie" he muttered.

"Have you broken down Sean?" she asked innocently. Before he could answer she continued, "I'll get my daddy."

"No, Rosie!" stated Sean, rather sharply. "I mean, I haven't broken down. I was just waiting here because . . . . I wanted to see you."

"Why?" asked Rosie, "is there anything wrong? . . . . Is Jim OK?" She was instantly anxious.

"Yes, he's fine," replied Sean, "why don't you get into the car for a minute, I just want to talk to you." Rosie felt a moment's relief when she heard that Jim was OK. This was replaced almost as quickly by a sense of panic. Somehow she knew what Sean was going to say to her. She knew it was about Jim going away and she was filled with terror.

After Rosie got into the car Sean started to drive slowly. He turned, after a minute, towards Lough Neagh, but remained silent. Rosie could not bring herself to speak. She was full of foreboding, and dreaded what she knew to be inevitable. She longed to jump out of the car so she would not have to hear what Sean had to say. Finally, after what seemed like an age, Sean pulled the car into a secluded gateway and turned off the engine.

"Rosie," he began slowly, "you know, I think you're a real nice girl and I know Jim really *likes* you, ... but there is something I have to say to you." He had emphasised the word likes in a way that made it sound like an insult. Rosie was deeply wounded. She became defensive.

"What's that Sean?" she asked, as sarcastically as she could manage.

It was Sean's turn to become anxious. Having started the conversation he could not find the right words to continue it. He settled for using the wrong ones.

"I don't think you should see our Jim anymore. He's supposed to be going to America at the end of the month and you're kinda gettin' in the way of his plans."

Rosie absorbed this statement for a moment before replying, "Are they his plans or *your* plans I'm getting in the way of Sean?"

Her words stung him, but he was in no mood for backing down.

"Rosie, can't you see that it's the right thing for him to do. If he stays here we're all worried that he'll end up in the Provies."

"Well you're not in the Provies', nor is any of the rest of your family. Why do you think Jim's about to run off and join the IRA? He's not stupid you know."

"I know that Rosie, but . . . . things have happened . . . . and Jim is at that age where he could end up getting involved even if he doesn't want to."

Rosie was not convinced. She, like the rest of her family, had been largely protected from much of the reality of the situation in Northern Ireland. Politics were never discussed at home, and Rosie had only a dim awareness of the social inequalities and religious prejudices which had led to the outbreak of war in the country. Growing up it had been impossible to ignore the daily news reports, and the more obvious injustices and prejudices which existed in Northern Ireland. However Rosie, like many of her generation, had grown tired of the rhetoric and sick of the carnage. She liked to believe that one day Protestants and Catholics would be able to live in peace with each other. Rosie even had a Protestant boyfriend called Sam for several weeks the year before. While she was going out with him, Mr and Mrs Maguire had experienced many hours of anxiety. Rosie had refused to acknowledge any problem with seeing a fella from the *other side* of town: blindly ignoring the danger she placed herself and Sam in every time she visited him at his home. Both Sam and Rosie's parents were very much relieved when the relationship ended. Sam cried when Rosie told him it was over. He accused her of being a bigot, which had wounded her deeply. The reality was that, being infatuated with Jim O'Loan, Rosie tended to lose interest in other boyfriends very quickly. She had simply tired of Sam and could see no reason to prolong the annoyance of her parents. Rosie believed that she had made her point. She was most certainly not a bigot.

"Does Jim know you're here?" asked Rosie. She was mortified at the idea that Jim might have told his brother to talk to her.

"No, he doesn't, ... and I don't want you to tell him" replied Sean. "I just want you to listen to me Rosie," he continued, "if Jim knew I was here he'd be raging . . . . I just need you to understand that if he misses out on going to America he . . . well . . . . he might blame you one day. Maybe you two will end up together Rosie, but after a while he's going to wonder what it would have been like if he'd gone to the States." Rosie thought for a moment. Sean's blatant lack of tact enabled her to consider what he said without wondering about his motives. It was clear he did not care about her feelings', only about what was right for his brother. Her thoughts were already racing ahead imaging the years of misery without Jim. Turning to Sean she said, "OK, I understand that he should go, but what do you want me to do? If he wants to go he'll go; if he wants to stay he'll stay. I can't make him do anything, can I?" Rosie sounded like a child. She knew that both she and Jim had been avoiding the topic for weeks and that, for her part, she had managed to bury her head in the sand so deeply that she had convinced herself that Jim didn't want to go to America anymore. She realised now that there was more to consider than what either of them wanted at that moment. Rosie had some pride. She could not bear to think of Jim resenting her or blaming her for keeping him in Ireland. Her love was not of the self sacrificing kind, but she was wise enough to see that to win now was to lose ultimately.

"I want you to tell him to go Rosie. That's all you need to do. If you tell him he should go it will be easier for him to make the decision. If you don't say anything he will just keep putting it off until it's too late." Rosie could say nothing. She felt as if she was suffocating. She wanted to get out of the car and run away and pretend she had never spoken with Sean. Slowly she turned to face him,

"I will tell him to go Sean . . . . can you bring me home now?" Sean started the car.

"Of course Rosie," he said. Having managed to convince Rosie to let Jim go; Sean did not feel good. He felt as if he had just broken something precious. He could not bear to look at Rosie. She was sitting silently beside him. He wanted to hold her. He continued to drive in silence until they reached her house. As she went to get out of the car, his words stopped her momentarily,

"You're a fine girl Rosie."

"Good bye Sean" she said looking at him. Her eyes were glazed, her expression stony. At that moment she hated Sean O'Loan, and he knew it.

Chapter Six

Rosie was not due to see Jim again until Tuesday night. She had spent the previous forty-eight hours mulling over what Sean had said and preparing herself for her next encounter with Jim. He was calling for her at 8 o'clock. She was so anxious by the time he arrived that Jim was shocked by her expression when she opened the door.

"What's the matter Rosie?" he asked, as she shut the door behind her and walked silently to his car.

"Nothing!" she replied, attempting to sound casual. Jim was not convinced. He immediately began to worry that she now regretted what had happened on the previous Friday night. It was clearly her first time, and Jim had been as gentle as he could. He wondered if he had hurt her. He then wondered if she was pregnant. He could barely contain the panic this thought instilled in him. For a brief moment he considered running away. Automatically he opened the car door for her then got into the car himself. He started the engine without speaking and, reversing out of the drive, he turned towards town. It was several minutes before he spoke.

"Rosie, is there anything you want to tell me?" he finally said.

"Yes, Jim, there is . . . . but it's not what you think. I'm not pregnant."

Jim almost stalled the car as the wave of relief flowed over him. *Thank you Jesus!* he thought to himself.

It took Jim a moment to realise that Rosie had not told him what was wrong. He decided to stop the car before asking her. He pulled into the marina, the scene of their first date, and parked the car in a secluded part of the car park.

"What's wrong Rosie?" he asked, after switching the engine off and turning towards her. Rosie was looking straight ahead. She bent her head down and away from him before answering,

"I don't think we should see each other any more Jim," she said.

"What?" demanded Jim, instantaneously surprised and bewildered, "Why not?" he continued, staring at her in disbelief. Rosie turned to him and said quietly,

"Well Jim, I don't think either of us can afford to fly between New York and Tullybeg every week . . . . and you know long distance relationships don't tend to last . . . . I mean I went out with a fella from Dublin one time and we only saw each other about once a month. Imagine how hard it would be to keep in touch if you're on the other side of the Atlantic?"

"Who says I'm going to New York?" Jim asked, defiantly.

"You did . . . . when we first starting going out . . . . remember?"

"Yeah, well maybe I changed my mind."

"Well, *you better change it back or we will both be sorry*" sang Rosie, quoting from the No 1 song in her best English accent, which was awful. Jim could not help but smile.

"Why are you saying this now Rosie, we haven't talked about this in weeks and I thought it was forgotten about . . . . it seems that everyone wants me to get rid of me now."

"Well, you can be a bit of a pain Jim" Rosie said, attempting to lighten the mood, "and I'm actually really quite bored with you."

"You know, you are one wee bitch" he replied, before grabbing her by the shoulders and forcing her to look at him. He stared at her until her eyes filled with tears.

"I know you love me, Rosie," he said quietly.

"Evidently not as much as you love yourself" she said sarcastically. Jim was starting to get angry.

"Stop it Rosie!" he snapped. "I want to know what's going on here . . . . is this about Friday night? You know we don't have to do it again if you don't want to."

She pulled away from him and got out of the car. He followed her; grabbing her hand he spun her around until she faced him. She wanted to throw her arms around his neck and tell him she did love him, but Rosie was already immersed in the drama of the moment. She felt as if she was in an old black and white film, acting the greatest role of her life. Liszt's Liebestraum No.3 in A flat major began thumping in her head and she could not help but smile at the melodrama of it all.

"I think you should go to America Jim" she said sadly. "It's what you want to do, and I don't want to be blamed for holding you back".

"Is that what this is all about Rosie?" Jim demanded. "What age do you think I am that I can't make a decision about my own life without other people telling me what I should do?" he asked. Rosie looked at him.

"I'm not telling you what you should do Jim . . . . and I don't WANT you to go, but I can't be responsible for you staying here either . . . . you know I'll be going to Queen's next year. What then? Are you going to sit around and wait for me to come home every weekend?"

Jim was not able to answer her. He had not considered that Rosie might have future plans which did not involve him. He had been quietly confident for some time now that she loved him. He had assumed that any decisions regarding their future lay with him. It was for him to decide whether to stay or to go. It was for him to decide if their relationship ended or not. It slowly began to dawn on him that Rosie might have an alternate future plotted out for herself that did not involve him. His pride was hurt and, more than that, he felt something akin to self doubt. Would she really be able to walk away from their relationship with such apparent ease? He felt foolish. For some time now, he had been having an on-going inner debate with himself on the question of what to do about Rosie. Although it caused him much anxiety he always assumed that he was the decider. If Rosie finished with him now he would, of course, go to America. He realised that there would be nothing to keep him in Ireland. He could not help but feel a certain amount of relief. He no longer had a decision to make.

"I never thought of it like that Rosie," he said finally. "I suppose I was just thinking about myself and what I should do."

"You're a fella, Jim. That's what fellas do!" she replied, smiling.

Jim looked at her as if he was seeing her for the first time.

"You're suddenly very grown up Miss Rosaleen Maguire," he said, as he reached out and fixed a single strand of hair behind her ear. Rosie was electrified by his sudden gentleness and the unexpected feel of his touch. She stepped back slightly, unable to hold his gaze. Looking at the ground she replied,

"I think I've just aged considerably Mr O'Loan."

Jim reached out his arms to her and she stumbled forward into his embrace. He felt her body slump against him. She was trembling. He could sense the emotion rising within her frame and spilling out in silent tears.

"I love you Rosie" he said quietly. Her body tensed at his words, but she remained silent.

"Did you hear me, Rosie" he continued, "I love you."

"I know Jim . . . . I love you too" she replied, choking down her tears.

"Will you wait for me?" he asked, tilting her chin up so he could monitor her response.

She looked at him longingly, for a moment, before her expression changed. She smiled at him.

"No Jim, I don't think so," she said. Turning away she started to laugh,

"Jim I find it hard waiting for a bus, I'm very impatient you know." She turned back to face him and saw the stricken expression on his face. She knew she had hurt him. It was wrong to joke at a moment like this.

"If . . . I mean WHEN you go to America, I want you to go free. I want you to do all the things you planned to do before we started going out together. I don't want you to feel tied down . . . . when you come back maybe we'll be together again. I'd like that . . . but I'm not going to stop living my life while you're off enjoying yours".

Jim was amazed at her words. He could scarcely believe she was talking to him in this way. He was not aware that she had planned her speech for two days prior to their meeting.

During that time she rehearsed in her head every word she would say, and anticipated every possible response he might make.

"You're totally heartless Rosie Maguire. I bet you can't wait to get rid of me so you can be off with someone else. Is that it? Have you met somebody else?"

"Yes Jim, that's it . . . . I've been seeing a southern gentleman for some time now" she replied, feigning guilt.

"Who is he?" Jim demanded to know, "where does he live and what time does he get out of his work?"

"His name is Rhett Butler and he lives in Charleston!" snapped Rosie. She was beginning to grow weary of her starring role.

"That's a fuckin' queer name, that is!" snarled Jim. "Free State bastard!"

It dawned on Rosie suddenly that Jim had no idea who Rhett Butler was. He thought she was serious when she said she was seeing someone else. Jim rarely cursed in front of her and he always apologised when he did.

"Jim, I was only joking, Rhett Butler doesn't exist. He's from *Gone with the Wind*! Remember? Clark Gable?"

"Oh," said Jim, suddenly calming down, "I see. Well how was I supposed to know? That's a girls' film."

"Actually it was a Pulitzer Prize winning novel first, you philistine," replied Rosie. She held her hand out to him and stroked his chest.

"I'm sorry Jim, I was only trying to make it easier for you," she muttered, hoping to calm him down. He began to laugh.

"I'm not really into watching films, or reading that much. Never have time" he muttered by way of an explanation. He was embarrassed by his ignorance.

Rosie smiled at him. He was the epitome of maleness which she loved, but she could not help regretting that he was not able to appreciate her wit. She wanted to make him understand her, but realised that this would never be entirely possible.

"Well, I think that's what you should do when you're in New York," she said. "You should sit in every night and read and watch telly and not go out. You should definitely not go out with any America girls. I hear they all have herpes!"

Jim could not help laughing. Even her feigned jealousy made him feel good. He knew that she would break her heart over him leaving. Knowing this, he felt that he could go to his new life in the States without too much regret for what might have been. What better monument to their love than the thought of Rosie back home heart broken and pining for him? He suddenly felt magnificent.

Rosie felt like shit. Her head was thumping and she did not feel able to keep up the charade for much longer.

"Jim, will you take me home" she said quietly. Her miserable face and red eyes brought Jim back down to earth. He suddenly recalled that he and Rosie were breaking things off and that he was not going to see her again for a long time. Why had he been feeling so elated? How did Rosie always manage to make him feel so confused? Had he really agreed to go to America and leave her? Had he actually had any real say in the matter? It began to dawn on him that he had been somehow manipulated again.

"Sure Rosie, you look . . . tired".

"I am" she said, "I feel like I've been run over by a bus."

"I'm sorry Rosie . . . you know I wish you could come with me to America".

She suddenly smiled,

"Be careful what you wish for Jim, it may come true!"

"Will you write to me?" he asked her. They had reached the car again and, as he opened the door for her she replied,

"Yes dear, as soon as you learn to read!"

"Bitch!" said Jim.

When they arrived back at Rosie's house, Jim drove the car into the driveway and turned off the ignition. He waited for Rosie to say something but she remained silent. She was paralysed by the intensity of her feelings and did not trust herself to speak. It was left to Jim to break the silence.

"Can I see you again before I leave Rosie?" he asked. This was one of the many questions Rosie had anticipated in her preparations for their final meeting. She knew that she would not be able to hold it together much longer and was therefore decisive in her response,

"No, Jim, this is doing my head in."

Jim was surprised at the sharpness of her reply until he noticed the tears in her eyes.

"Off course, Rosie, what ever you think love" he responded in his kindest voice. It was too much for Rosie. She burst into floods of tears, quickly kissed him on the cheek, wished him 'goodbye and good luck' before jumping out of the car, slamming the door and running inside the house. Jim was left reeling. He wanted to follow her. He wanted his *long goodbye*. She had deprived him of this. He felt cheated. Turning on the engine of the car he slowly reversed out of the driveway and out onto the road.

"Fuck sake!" he muttered to himself, slamming the palms of his hands hard onto the steering wheel.

Chapter Seven

It was the 1st September 1984 when the Boeing 747 carrying Jim to his new life landed in JFK Airport. The long flight was made endurable by the attention lavished on him by the *Aer Lingus* air hostesses. As he was an attractive male, sitting alone, the younger attendants flirted outrageously with him and the older ones mothered him mercilessly. He was plied with alcohol, and consequently Jim arrived in New York pluthered. Walking unsteadily he only just managed to retrieve his baggage from the carousel before staggering out into the arrival area of the airport. Cousin Mary was waiting anxiously for him. When she finally recognised Jim she screamed his name and ran forward to greet him.

Mary Magee was the daughter of Jim's uncle John: his mother's brother. She was twenty seven years old and had been living in New York for almost five years. She hugged Jim affectionately. Noticing the smell of alcohol she pulled away from him and announced to the world in general,
"You're pissed Jim O'Loan! The last time I saw you, you were this height!" She indicated with the flat of her hand a distance of some three feet of the floor,

"Now look at the size of you, and drinking too like a big man!" Jim beamed at her and finally managed to say, "Hiya Mary, ssgood to sthee you!" Mary laughed at him. "Let's get you home before you fall over" she said. They walked towards the exit, Jim carrying his case, Mary linking his arm, partly from the deep affection she felt for him and partly because she was afraid he would make a spectacle of himself by falling over. They hailed a cab. It was 10 o'clock in the morning and the traffic was heavy. Despite his inebriated state Jim still managed to take in much of his surroundings. He was disappointed that there were no skyscrapers. Mary explained to him that he would have to travel into Manhattan to see real skyscrapers.

Mary lived in Jackson Heights in the borough of Queens, in a second storey apartment she shared with her boyfriend Stan. Stan was a native New Yorker, born and raised in Queens. His parents lived two blocks away. The journey back to the apartment took over an hour because of the heavy traffic and, when they finally arrived, Jim was feeling nauseous. Mary showed him to his room and advised him to lie down. Before she could finish making him a cup of coffee, Jim was fast asleep and snoring loudly. Mary covered him with a blanket and left him to sleep off his alcohol induced stupor.

When he awoke, several hours later, Jim was feeling bad. He opened his eyes wincing at the daylight streaming through the open window. His head thumped and his mouth was rough as a badger's ass. He glanced at his watch. It was one o'clock in the morning, Irish time. He reckoned it must be at least 7 o'clock in the evening New York time.

Throwing off the blanket, Jim got out of bed and made his way into the main living area of the apartment. He could smell dinner cooking and was reminded instantly of his belly. He wandered into the small kitchen where Mary was stirring something on the cooker. Beside her stood the most enormous man Jim had ever seen. He was at least six and half feet tall. Jim was rendered speechless. The man had a small beard and wore John Lennon type glasses. He noticed Jim standing in the door way with his mouth open before Mary did. The huge man introduced himself,

"Hi, I'm Stan, Mary's boyfriend." Shaking hands with him, Jim immediately felt that this was a character he would like to get to know. Stan was a gentle giant and, judging by the twinkle in his eyes, he was also a bit of a joker.

Mary told Jim to sit down while she finished making dinner. After some minutes, during which Jim chatted to Stan, Mary handed him a large plate of spaghetti with meatballs. Jim was ravenous but was not familiar with the technicalities of eating this particular dish. He had been brought up on a diet of potatoes, meat and vegetables. Pasta was a relatively new experience for him. After managing the first two mouthfuls successfully; he was an instant convert, and complimented Mary on her cooking. She smiled graciously before handing Stan his dinner and getting her own plate. They chatted while eating their meal. Mary was keen to catch up on news off family back home. The conversation turned eventually to the death of young Mark O'Loan whom Mary had known as a young boy. Jim told the story of his death briefly with little apparent emotion. He had relived the incident many times in his head and was, by now, able to disguise his true feeling regarding the loss of Mark. Mary noticed the strain in Jim's face as he finished talking. She decided to lighten the tone of the conversation and, in typical older woman fashion, began to tease Jim about *the girls back home*. Jim's face coloured instantly and he was rendered speechless. He had not thought about Rosie for several hours, and had not seen her for nearly two weeks. He was missing her terribly already. The past forty eight hours in particular had been hell. He had been torn between the excitement of his imminent journey and the heart rending decision to leave Rosie. He could not think about her now without feeling an intense pain which, not only took him by surprise but, brought back to him the grief he had experienced following Mark's death. Mary noticed Jim's sadness. She was a sensitive girl and she missed her own family enormously. The only thing keeping her in New York was the love she felt for Stan. Mary patted Jim on the shoulder and said lightly,

"Maybe we'll get you introduced to a nice Yankee girl, while you're over here, and you can settle down and raise a brood of youngsters with American accents!" Jim smiled. The thought horrified him! It was not that he expected never to marry and have children. Rather he assumed that he would, but definitely not for many, many years yet. He looked at Mary coyly and responded,

"I think you're the one who'll be settling down with the Yank and breeding youngsters." He looked at Stan who was overcome with shyness at the allusion to marriage. He was currently saving desperately to buy Mary an engagement ring; he lived in constant dread that she would return to Ireland before he built up the nerve to pop the question. Mary shuffled about clearing the table while she laughed. Thumping Jim on the shoulder she replied giggling,

"Sure I'm far too young to be getting married!"

The conversation eventually turned to what Jim might do in the way of finding himself employment. Mary insisted there was no need for him to rush. He should enjoy the sights of New York first and have a bit of a holiday to himself. She and Stan were both working, and he was more than welcome to stay with them for as long as he wanted. Jim thanked them both for the kind offer but he made it clear from the start that, as soon as he found employment, he would be seeking alternative accommodation. He did not expect them to keep him for more than a few weeks. He had some savings which his mother had deducted from his wages every week since he was fourteen years of age. He had also sold his car before coming to New York which had paid for his flight and then some. Jim was aware that without a social security number the type of work available to him would be limited. He was a skilled plasterer and a competent enough joiner, but his skill and experience meant nothing if he could not work legally. Mary said she might be able to get him a start in the bar where she worked. Jim had no experience of working in bars and the thought of it scared him. He did not admit this to Mary. Stan suggested he try labouring on a building site to begin with. Jim was not above labouring. He remembered (with some regret) the years he spent as an apprentice on building sites being taunted by the older men. He also remembered how he, in turn, had tortured his own apprentice, when he had finally been allocated one. It would be like starting over again.

After a while Jim asked if he could take a shower. He was feeling grubby and his clothes smelled of smoke and sweat.

Mary suggested that, after he had washed and changed, they might go out for a drink to their local. Stan was enthusiastic and, though the thought of drinking at that moment made Jim feel sick, he was more than happy to begin his New York experience in a bar. He washed quickly and dressed in his best shirt and trousers. Mary laughed when she saw him,

"We're not going to the Plaza just yet Jim, you can wear your jeans you know." Jim was relieved. He quickly changed into an old pair of Levis and, grabbing a jacket, followed Stan and Mary out into the night air. The three of them chatted warmly as they made their way onto Roosevelt Avenue. After walking for a few blocks, they eventually stopped at a brightly lit bar displaying a large neon shamrock announcing it to be an Irish bar. Jim thought it weird that he had travelled five thousand miles from Ireland to go drinking in an Irish pub. Stepping inside he instantly recognised that particular smell peculiar to bars throughout the world, the smell of smoke, stale and fresh; sweat (also stale and fresh); beer; and that other significant ingredient, essential to bars all over the world, life itself. The odour hit him in the face evoking memories of hundreds of previous evenings spent drinking with friends in pubs. He felt excited and alive. The place was buzzing but in a subdued way. A duke box was playing *The Pogues* in the background, and in the rear of the bar Jim could see a pool table where a handful of young men gathered to watch two opponents play. Stan got the drinks in, while Mary ushered Jim to a seat at the bar. Before long Jim was introduced to several of his hosts' friends. The atmosphere was pleasant and he felt instantly relaxed. He managed to gulp down his first beer with relative ease and before long he was looking forward to another. The *hair of the dog* that bit him was working its magic. Jim was feeling good.

In the course of the evening, Jim made several useful contacts who promised to help him get work. Later on, lying in bed he felt positive that he would find employment soon. Jim was not used to being out of work. He was an early riser and enjoyed feeling useful.
He fell asleep quickly that night and dreamt of Rosie and his mother. Both women were crying in the dream. He could not make them stop no matter what he said or did. It was as if they could not see him.

When he awoke the next morning, Jim could hear movement in the apartment. He jumped out of bed instantly, worried that Mary and Stan might think he was used to lying in bed. He dressed quickly and went into the kitchen where Stan was pouring freshly brewed coffee. Jim preferred tea but gratefully accepted the beverage on offer. Over the course of the next couple of months Jim was to grow addicted to coffee. Now it tasted bitter but it quenched his thirst immediately. Both Mary and Stan worked locally and were getting ready to leave. It was almost 8 o'clock. Mary gave Jim a key to the apartment and handed him a note book in which she had written her home address and phone number along with her work address and number. Mary advised him that he should travel into Manhattan on the subway. She offered to show him where to get the train on her way to work. After gathering up his wallet and a small camera, Jim left the apartment with Stan and Mary.

Stan worked nearby for a furniture removal company. He enjoyed his work and was popular with his co-workers. He was in cheery mood. When they reached Roosevelt Avenue, Stan kissed Mary goodbye and said good luck to Jim. Mary and Jim turned right on Roosevelt Avenue and Stan turned left. Mary then gave Jim brief directions, in relation to the train, and advised him to get off the subway at the 5th Avenue stop in Manhattan. Jim was beginning to feel a bit anxious about walking around New York on his own. He had bought himself a guide book before leaving Ireland, which he had attempted to read on the plane prior to becoming intoxicated. He was familiar with certain names and places and understood that there were five boroughs in New York City: Queens being one and Manhattan another. It was Manhattan that he was anxious to see.

Stepping off the subway at the 5th Avenue exit, Jim's heart began to race. He was being ushered along by the crowds of commuters; his feet barely touched the ground before he was propelled out of the exit of the station and into the brightness of the September morning. The experience was exhilarating. This was the New York of films. Doing a complete 360 degree turn, Jim was bombarded by the sights and sounds of Manhattan in morning time. He was awestruck. After several minutes, he began to look skyward; only then did he notice the immenseness of the skyscrapers. It made him feel dizzy at first. Nearby he noticed a news paper stand; as he was unsure which way was uptown and which way was downtown, he decided to ask the newspaper seller for directions. When he spoke, the man's eyes flickered with recognition,

"You Irish?" he stated. Jim responded in the affirmative. The man seemed pleased to share his knowledge of his native city. He gave Jim a street map and provided him with a brief lesson on its use. He pointed out downtown, towards the Empire State Building, and advised Jim that he was within easy walking distance of this particular monument to the audacity of man. He told Jim not to keep his camera or his map too visible as this instantly identified him as a tourist. He also gave Jim a lesson on the use of buses and how to avoid getting *taken for a ride* by cab drivers. Jim thanked the man for his help and saying good bye set off downtown on foot.

After several blocks Jim reached the entrance to the Empire State Building. It was only just after 10.00 o'clock in the morning, but the place was already a hive of activity with tourists milling around taking photographs of the exquisite art deco décor or waiting to enter the elevator to the viewing gallery. When the doors of the elevator opened, Jim stepped aside to allow an elderly couple access before he too entered. They smiled at him and continued to make small talk. Jim's heart leaped as the elevator commenced its journey skyward. He was overwhelmed with excitement. On reaching the viewing gallery, Jim headed straight outside. He was not interested in souvenirs. He wanted to see around him. He was not disappointed. The view from the top of the Empire State Building had to be one of the most magnificent in the world. Jim was astounded at how far he could see and the minuteness of the buildings below, many of which were substantial skyscrapers in their own right. Looking downtown towards the World Trade Centre he could see the distinctive twin towers rising out of the landscape and pointing out the Statue of Liberty beyond. The top of the Chrysler Building glittered in the morning sun. Jim thought it was magnificent.

As he looked in awe at the sprawling city below, Jim experienced a deep sense of sadness. He knew instinctively that Rosie was thinking of him at that moment. He knew also that she would love to see what he was seeing and to experience what he was experiencing. He wished she was with him now. He wanted to show the world to her and to show her to the world. He knew at that moment that his life would never be complete without her. No experience, no other woman, no job, no amount of money, nor freedom could replace what he had left behind him in Ireland. He began to feel something akin to hysteria. He had heard about women having hysterics or fainting fits or being *overcome with emotion.* He realised then that this must be what it was like. He looked around him furtively to see if anyone had noticed his feelings. He was almost convinced that people could hear what he was thinking. He wanted to fly off the building and get home to Rosie right away. He remained rooted to the spot, unable to move and silenced by convention. If he had been alone, he would have howled like a wolf to relieve the pain he felt inside. After several minutes, during which he lectured himself inwardly about *pulling himself together* and *being a man*, Jim finally felt strong enough to move. After taking one final glance around him, he made his way to the elevator and descended to the ground floor. He found the elevator claustrophobic and the chatter of its passengers irritating. He practically ran out of the building and gasped for air upon reaching the street outside. He attracted the notice of several passers by, but no one stopped to ask if he was OK. Had he behaved like this at home, he was sure at least one person would have stopped to offer their assistance. It was one of the many ironies about life in Northern Ireland. Despite the desire of several of its inhabitants to blow each other up, there remained an old-fashioned sense of community and concern for your fellow beings that had long since disappeared from more sophisticated societies.

Jim decided that he needed some refreshment. He noticed a bar beside the entrance to the Empire State Building, heading straight for the door he walked in and sat down on a bar stool. Jim felt it was too early for a beer so he ordered a coffee. It seemed the New York thing to do. When the bar tender served the coffee Jim poured sugar into it and stirred it continually for several seconds. He took a long sip and began to feel better. He wanted peace to gather his thoughts. He knew he would look foolish if he went running back to Ireland now. He should at least give New York a chance. He decided he would find a job first, get his own place, and then he would ask Rosie to come to New York to be with him. She might say no, but at least he would know how she really felt about him. Jim was barely able to admit to himself the strength of his feelings for Rosie. He was unsure if he would ever be able to admit them to Rosie. She had talked about going to university and about seeing other men. Perhaps she had already gotten over him? Perhaps she was already dating someone else? The idea of Rosie being with another man infuriated Jim. He grew angry and without thinking thumped his fist on the bar, almost knocking his coffee flying. The bar tender, who had been watching Jim approached him quietly and asked if he was OK.

"I'm fine," replied Jim, "just arguing with myself."

"You know there are places for people like you" said the bar tender looking curiously at Jim. Jim was about to take serious offence at this remark when he noticed the man smirking at him. He also noticed a very slight hint of a Northern Irish accent. It was barely perceptible, but it was there.

"Are you taking the piss?" enquired Jim. The bar tender began to laugh.

"Of course" he replied, "I'm from Northern Ireland, that's what we do best!"

"You're right there" laughed Jim. "where abouts are you from?"

"I'm from Derry. You?"

"Armagh".

"Ach well," the Derry man sympathised, "sure we can't help where we're born!"

"Fuck you!" said Jim and both men began to laugh.

The bartender's name was Micheal. He told Jim that he'd been living in New York for six years and he had his own apartment in Jackson Heights in Queens. Jim instantly liked the man. Micheal had managed to retain most of his Northern Irish sense of humour and the two men hit it off from the start. Michael was saving to go home. He wanted to earn enough money to start his own business in Ireland. He wanted to buy property there. He was renting his apartment at the moment and, after hearing Jim's plans, he offered to sublet him a room. Jim was suspicious at first that a virtual stranger would offer to share his place with him.

He looked at Michael warily. Michael was not offended. He simply said that it made sense. They could share the rent and bills and this would allow him to save more towards his ultimate goal of going home.

Jim pointed out that he had not yet found work.

"Sure you only arrived yesterday, I'm sure I could hold the room . . . . for a day or two . . . until you get yourself sorted" said Michael.

Jim was not so sure.

"I don't even know where to start looking for work" he muttered.

Michael asked what sort of work he could do. When Jim told him he was a time served plasterer; Michael was impressed,

"Sure I know a fella would get you a start right away."

"But I don't have a green card or anything" said Jim.

"You leave that to me, if you're willing to pay for it you can get anything in this town."

It was Jim's turn to be impressed. He had been in New York for less than forty-eight hours and already it looked like he was going to get himself a job and a place to live. He started to feel more positive. Perhaps he could stick it out for a while.

Chapter Eight

Less than two weeks later, Jim was sitting in the apartment he shared with Michael writing a letter to Rosie. He was feeling optimistic. Though he still missed Rosie, he was now hopeful that things may work out for the best. He thought long and hard before committing his thoughts to paper,

Dear Rosie,

I'm sorry I haven't been in touch. I've been busy trying to get work. I finally started a job yesterday on a building site.

New York is huge but I think I have seen just about everything. Liberty was asking for you! Anyway, I've just moved in with a fella from Derry and we get on the best. I have my own room. Michael works long hours so I have the place to myself a lot.

I'm hoping to get my own place soon. I want you to come over and stay with me when I do. You'll love it here. I really miss you. I suppose you're already going out with some one else? If you are

I'll understand but I want you to know that I still love you. Please write and let me know what you think about coming over here.

Love Jim

When Rosie received Jim's letter she began to shake. It had been over four weeks since he had departed from her life. Rosie had suffered unimaginably. The letter arrived on a Saturday morning and she tore it opened as soon as Kate threw it on her bed. Despite already being late for her Saturday job, Rosie refused to get out of bed before reading the letter three times from beginning to end. Every word inspired her with feelings of intense joy coupled with excruciating pain. *He still loved her. He still wanted her.* All Rosie's doubts evaporated and were replaced with an intense need to be reunited with Jim. The miles between them were unbearable and, not for the first time, Rosie experienced the desire to hurt Sean O'Loan (whom she blamed entirely for her enforced separation from Jim). She wished she had never listened to him. She wished she had told him to go to hell and back before agreeing to finish with Jim. What did he know about love? What did he care about the pain he had inflicted on her and his brother? He was cruel. She could not think of anything bad enough to wish on Sean. She wanted him to die. Then she felt guilty and, after hurriedly saying an Act of Contrition, she reduced his imaginary sentence to a lifetime of abject misery. After finishing the letter, Rosie jumped out of bed. She had made a decision. She was going to New York to be with Jim as soon as she turned eighteen. It was four months until her birthday. She would need to start saving right away. *Better get to work before I get fired* she thought.

Rosie enjoyed her job. She worked in a chip shop in Tullymore from 9 o'clock in the morning until six in the evening every Saturday. During the school holidays she had been working almost full time. The chip shop was owned by a family of Italians and they also sold the best homemade ice cream in the world. Rosie was addicted to it. If she had been offered her wages in Morellie's ice cream she would probably have accepted it. Mostly however, it was the buzz in the shop she enjoyed. The place was always packed with shoppers and young people meeting to share a chip and a chat. When she arrived at work, Rosie put her bicycle in the shed at the back of the shop and walked into the kitchen. Her boss, Tony Morrellie, looked at his watch as she passed him,
"Late again, Rosie!" he said, looking sternly at her.
"Ah, you see, it was like this Tony . . . ." she began. Before she could continue, Tony Morrellie began to laugh,
"I don't want to hear it Rosie, your stories always make me cry!"
Rosie smiled. She liked Tony; he was kind and treated his staff with respect. He had taught Rosie just about all there was to know about the fast food business and he had frequently relied on Rosie to mind the shop when he was away. Despite the fact that she had been working for most of the summer, Rosie had managed to save only a fraction of her wages. She thought about asking Tony for a full time job so she could save her fare to New York. She was sure he would agree. The problem would be to convince her parents to allow her to leave school.

Rosie was in the final year of studying for her 'A' levels. She was not a particularly good student. She loved to read, but studying was a different matter. While doing her 'O' levels, when she should have been revising, Rosie had read *Gone with the Wind*. Unable to set the novel down, she had badly neglected her studies and just managed to scrape eight exam passes. She had excelled in maths and English. The rest of her results were Cs. Rosie was doing English literature, ancient history and maths for 'A' level subjects. She had read all of the English novels required at least twice and in the case of *Wuthering Heights* she had memorised full passages and knew the book well. She also loved Shakespeare; *Anthony and Cleopatra* was her favourite play. Overall, there was a good chance that Rosie would pass her English literature 'A' level with relative ease: not so ancient history. Rosie had managed to miss as many classes as possible. She had wanted to learn about ancient history because she had always been fascinated by Greek mythology. She had also read Homer's Iliad and Odyssey and loved the stories. In reality ancient history, as studied at 'A' level, had greatly disappointed Rosie. She generally ceased paying attention in class after the first fifteen minutes. Her ancient history teacher now referred to her as 'you there' as he was unable to remember her name given her frequent absences from class.

Unfortunately maths 'A' level was also proving to be a problem. Rosie was a natural mathematician and loved maths from an early age. As a child she enjoyed doing algebra just for fun. The difficulty was that Rosie clashed horribly with her new maths teacher. Miss Kelly was a young and relatively attractive woman with slightly horsy features and a nasally voice which irritated Rosie. Rosie had made the huge *faux pas* of pointing out a mistake in her calculations when she had been attempting to solve a complicated equation in front of the class. Miss Kelly had never forgiven her. Rosie was forced to sit at the front of the class under the teacher's direct observation and invariably she added insult to injury by falling asleep, while Miss Kelly (or *Ned* as Rosie called her behind her back) was attempting to teach. The rift between Rosie and *Ned* had widened considerably over the previous year to the point where Rosie no longer even bothered to hand in homework assignments. It was unlikely that Rosie would pass her maths 'A' level now, unless Miss Kelly was to be replaced by another, less sensitive soul.

Rosie was unable to consider her future plans for long as the shop was busy, and she was forced to work hard in the morning. She had arranged to meet Ellie in the pub next to the chip shop at 12 'o'clock (during her lunch break), and wanted to get her regular Saturday chores in the shop completed on time. Rosie was dying to tell Ellie about her letter from Jim. When the appointed time arrived Rosie told Tony she was going out for half an hour and, taking off her apron, she hurried out of the shop. Ellie was standing at the door of the pub waiting for her; she would not go into a public house on her own. After ordering a class of lemonade each, the girls sat down in a darkened corner and both lit up a cigarette. Rosie immediately launched into her tale of woe. Ellie listened. She had little choice. Rosie was on a roll. Ellie said nothing until Rosie announced that, given Jim's declaration, she had decided to leave school and go to New York in January when she turned eighteen. Ellie was struck dumb momentarily. After composing herself she said,

"Rosie, are you on drugs? You can't just leave school like that! Your ma and da'll kill you!"

"They can't kill me if I'm eighteen!" Rosie replied, petulantly.

"I could kill you now!" snapped Ellie. She was frequently amazed by Rosie's lack of sense but really believed that Rosie had now lost the plot entirely. Taking a deep breath she said,

"Well tell me this Rosie, where do you think you're getting the money to go to New York and what are you going to live on when you get there?" Ellie was talking to her as if she thought Rosie had spontaneously developed a severe learning difficulty.

"I can work full time in Morrellie's to earn the flight money and I can get a job when I get there. Jim's already working."

"So you're going to let a man keep you, are you?"

"It's not like that, Ellie. It's just till I get work."

"That's not the point, Rosie. You'll be living with a man and there'll be sex . . . . and all sorts. It'll kill your ma and da."

Rosie had not considered this aspect of the equation. She had assumed at some stage that she and Jim would get married. Living in sin was not her intention. As if reading her thoughts Ellie began to speak softly in a concerned tone, "Rosie, I know you love Jim, and perhaps he really does love you, but you can't just give up your life and your plans and go running half way across the world just because Jim O'Loan says he's missing you. What if you get over there and you and him have a fight or fall out. You'll be stuck there with no way of getting home . . . . it's not like you're married or anything."

"Well we could get married," replied Rosie, attempting to look optimistic.

"Has he asked you? Has he even mentioned it?" asked Ellie.

"No, but he does love me . . . . and I love him. What's more important than that?" stated Rosie defiantly.

"I'll tell you what's more important Rosie," said Ellie, looking her friend straight in the eye, "your self-respect and your independence. If you go to America now, you'll go as a dependent. You'll be going straight from your dad keeping you to Jim keeping you. Remember what we always talked about. Getting away from home and living independently: no one telling us what to do or when to come and go. If you shack up with Jim O'Loan *maybe* you two will get married and have babies . . . . but you'll never know what it's like to do your own thing. You'll be missing out on an awful lot Rosie for the sake of a fella."

"I'm missing out on an awful lot now Ellie" said Rosie quietly. "I can't sleep at night for thinking of him. It hurts all the time. I miss him so much I want to cry all the time."

Ellie felt very sorry for Rosie. She believed that Rosie was talking shite but she also knew that it was genuine shite. She did not know what else to say to her. Perhaps Rosie would be better going to New York and getting this thing out of her system. Maybe she and Jim would end up living happily ever after. Ellie doubted it, but she knew there was little more she could say to Rosie to make her change her mind. Rosie could be extremely determined when she wanted to be.

"Well Rosie, I have to go now," said Ellie, standing up and lifting her cigarettes and lighter from the table. She paused before she left,

"Will you at least talk to your ma and da before you go quitting school and booking your flight to New York?"

Rosie looked at her and smiled,

"Off course I will. I'm not eighteen until January. I've got plenty of time to talk them round." Ellie smiled half-heartedly. She had a dreadful sense of foreboding which unnerved her and made her want to grab Rosie and shake her until she came to her senses. She knew it would be futile however. She simply turned away calling,

"See you later!" to Rosie as she left the pub and wandered down the street towards home. Rosie hurried back to work. She was late again.

Chapter Nine

It took two weeks for Rosie to pluck up the courage to ask her parents if she could leave school and move to New York. Mrs Maguire laughed outright when Rosie announced her intentions. She assumed Rosie was joking. Her father treated Rosie's announcement more seriously. He automatically said 'no' but instinctively prepared himself for a battle. He knew that look on Rosie's face. It resembled his own whenever he was determined on a course of action. After much pleading and reasoning on Rosie's part, and attempts to 'talk some sense into her' on her parents part; the argument finally ended with Rosie's mother saying,

"No and that's final." Rosie stormed out of the room banging the door. They all knew it was not final. Rosie would be back with renewed vigour at some later stage.

For the time being she contented herself by attempting to make everyone else in the house as miserable as possible. Kate was called upon, at first, to provide a sympathetic ear, but when she pointed out to Rosie that she was acting like an idiot Kate was instantly dropped from service. Ann was even less sympathetic. When she came home from Queen's that weekend and heard about the fight between Rosie and her parents, Ann was initially prepared to listen to both sides. However, when Rosie launched into her monologue on the merits of being in love and the obvious need to pursue said love to the ends of the earth, Ann was left feeling cold and indifferent. She simply offered the following words of wisdom to her sister,

"Rosie, if you had decided to run away to join a hippy commune in San Francisco or to make a solo attempt on K2 or to join the circus you would have my total support, but to go running after a man who clearly left you to do his own thing I can neither understand nor condone. I am deeply disappointed in you Rosie." Rosie was completely confused by the adverse reaction of her family and friends to, what seemed to her, to be the perfect plan. She almost felt sorry for them. It was clear to her that none of them had any idea what it was like to be in love. She alone was privy to that experience. She believed that love was the only thing worth struggling for. She remained determined to leave school and go to America.

Ann returned to university on Sunday evening without attempting to talk to Rosie again. The following day Rosie caught the bus to school as usual. She did not speak to anyone during breakfast. Her mother was still extremely upset by Rosie's rantings, and everyone else appeared to be avoiding her. Shane had told his mother the night before that he was going to break Rosie's record player over her head if he had to listen to *Endless Love* or *Second Violin* once more. Mrs Maguire had wondered if she should let him. Rosie stared out of the window on the bus and gathered her thoughts. She was unable to think straight. Her desperation to be with Jim was overwhelming. She hated the thought of sitting in class listening to her teachers talk about subjects which she had long since cease to find even remotely interesting. When the bus arrived at school, Rosie was the last one to get off. It was raining heavily, and by the time Rosie reached the shelter of the building her duffle coat was saturated. The heavy wool material smelt *all rainy.* It reminded Rosie off being little and playing outside in all weathers. Rosie headed straight for the locker room in the basement of the building. All around her other young people were milling about talking and collecting books for their first class. The boys gathered around the radiators in the corridors soaking up what little heat there was and making smart comments to the girls as they passed by. Rosie smiled automatically at anyone who spoke to her but she was not listening. She felt as if she was in a trance being compelled along by an outside force unable to take control of her own limbs.

The first bell rang to announce it was time to go to form class for roll call. *Do not ask for whom the bell tolls,* thought Rosie as the ear piercing ring thundered through her head. She smiled to herself wondering if anyone would notice if she simply walked out of school and didn't come back. It struck her that no one could physically make her stay. She was over the legal age to leave school; even her parents could not make her go if she absolutely refused. Rosie's thoughts continued on this line for most of the morning. She barely answered any questions in English class. She was normally at the centre of any discussion; her English teacher eventually asked if she was feeling OK. Rosie lied and said she had a bit of a headache. She was subsequently left to her own thoughts.

After lunch Rosie had double maths class. The thought of it made her feel deeply depressed. Normally she survived this ordeal by day dreaming and escaping into her own world. However Miss Kelly appeared to be in even worse temper than normal, and Rosie knew instantly she would have to keep her wits about her in order to avoid a run in with the irascible *Ned*. Half way through the class Rosie became aware that *Ned* was circling her desk even more than usual. She sounded particularly nasally that day and Rosie winced every time she raised the pitch of her voice to emphasise a point. It seemed to Rosie that Miss Kelly was deliberately attempting to annoy her. Rosie wanted to swat her away like a fly. From the depths of her reverie Rosie was returned to reality by the sound of *Ned* calling her name sharply,

"Answer the question now Rosie" squeaked the teacher, in the most commanding voice she could muster.

"What question?" asked Rosie, genuinely unaware that Miss Kelly had spoken to her previously.

"I just asked you if you understood what I was saying," snapped Miss Kelly. Rosie had not been listening and was therefore unable to say yes.

"No Miss," she muttered. Not only had Miss Kelly anticipated this answer, but she appeared to welcome it. She knew Rosie had not been listening. It infuriated her. She wanted to humiliate Rosie. Rosie wanted to go back to her daydream. She was becoming uncomfortable having the attention of the entire class focused on her. Normally she would have tried to diffuse the situation by apologising, or asking Miss Kelly to repeat the question. Today Rosie felt reckless and angry. She could hardly bear to look at Miss Kelly. Her beady little eyes seemed to be boring holes into

Rosie's skin. She continued to fire questions at Rosie with a sadistic smirk on her face,

"I suppose Miss Maguire you think you don't need to listen in class. I suppose you think you know more than any of your teachers. Perhaps you think you should be up here teaching, and I should be sitting where you are?"

"No Miss" replied Rosie, her face growing redder by the second.

"Perhaps I should ask Sr. Mary Terese to join us? Maybe she might be able to interest you enough to keep you awake? Would you like me to go and get her now Rosie?" Rosie stared at her teacher. Miss Kelly looked triumphant. She was enjoying this. Rosie snapped. Standing up slowly she looked Miss Kelly in the eye,

"Frankly Ned, I don't give a flying fuck what you do!" said Rosie, before lifting her bag and walking slowly out of the class. For a moment everyone in the class, including Miss Kelly, remained dumbfounded. No one spoke. Gradually a quiet murmur arose until finally, some one was heard to laugh. The laughter shook Miss Kelly into action. She ordered the class to remain *seated and silent* then hurried out of the room in pursuit of Rosie.

Rosie had almost reached the front entrance of the school where the principal's office was situated when Miss Kelly caught up with her.

"Rosie Maguire, stop now!" she called. Rosie turned around to face her adversary. It was like a stand off in an old western film. Rosie imagined herself reaching for her gun, while the theme tune for *The Good, the Bad and the Ugly* played in her brain. The thought amused her. Her face became suddenly animated. The sound of Miss Kelly's voice caught the attention of Sr Mary Terese who was seated at her desk doing paperwork. She instantly got up and opened the door of the office,

"What's wrong Miss Kelly?" she enquired of the teacher who was almost white with rage by this stage. Miss Kelly was barely able to answer. She did not know where to begin. Looking at the principal, she managed to stammer,

"Rosie Maguire has just . . . used extremely foul language in my class . . . and then walked out."

The nun looked at Rosie, who remained rooted to the spot. "Is that true Rosie?" she asked.

"Yes sister" replied Rosie.

"Come into my office now!" commanded Sr Mary Terese, looking first at Rosie and then at Miss Kelly. They both walked into the room, Rosie's head hanging in shame, Miss Kelly holding hers high, prepared to defend herself to the hilt.

"Now please tell me what happened Miss Kelly" said the principal. Miss Kelly told a factual account of what had happened in the class. She added however, her own interpretation of Rosie's motives and feelings at the time and this, more than anything, enraged Rosie. When Miss Kelly finished talking Sr Mary Terese asked Rosie if what Miss Kelly said was true. Rosie had to admit that it was. She could not begin to explain the myriad nuances and petty differences that had plagued her relationship with Ned from day one. What was the point anyway? She had just used the 'F' word in class. Rosie knew that her days at school were numbered. She wanted it just to be over now. After all she wanted to leave any way. Sr Mary Terese stood up and advised Miss Kelly that she would deal with the matter now. Miss Kelly nodded obsequiously and shuffled out of the office. She gave Rosie a final glance that seemed to Rosie to epitomise her inner joy at having finally vanquished her enemy once and for all. Again Rosie imagined what it would be like to shoot her.

Sr Mary Terese told Rosie to take a seat and then sat down opposite her.

"Rosie, why did you behave like that in Miss Kelly's class?" she asked.

"I don't know" replied Rosie, looking at her feet.

"Well something must have happened to make you so angry" continued the older woman.

"She was just trying to show me up," said Rosie, "she was doing my head in".

"But why Rosie?"

"'cause she wouldn't shut up!"

"Rosie it is the teachers' job to teach in class, and your job to listen".

"Well I can't listen to her anymore. She sends me to sleep every time I'm in her class."

"Perhaps Rosie you just have too many other things on your mind at the moment."

Rosie glanced up at the principal. She wondered if Sr Mary Terese knew about her relationship with Jim. Could she see inside her soul? Did she know how unhappy she was? Sr Mary Terese smiled knowingly at Rosie. She had noticed the deterioration in Rosie's attitude and appearance over the past term and was concerned about it. Despite Rosie's many faults, Sr Mary Terese could not help but like the young girl. In many ways she reminded her of herself when she was that age. Sr Mary Terese had not always wanted to be a nun. She too had known love.

"It's got nothing to do with that" replied Rosie, "I just don't want to be here anymore but my mum and dad won't let me leave school."

"What do you want to do if you do leave school Rosie?"

"I want to work so I can save up the money to go to America in January when I'm eighteen."

"Have you got a job to go to now?"

"Yes in Morrellie's up the town".

"You know Rosie, I really think, even now, if you put you're mind to it, you could go to university next year."

"But I don't want to go to university . . . anymore."

"Why Rosie, what's changed?"

"I just don't want to go. I've got better things to do with my time than sitting round studying for the next four years. I want to get out into the real world and earn some money and have some fun."

"It's got nothing to do with that fella you were seeing over the summer then Rosie?"

"How did you know about Jim?" asked Rosie, really convinced now that this nun must have the ability to read minds.

"I didn't Rosie, but I think you just told me" replied Sr Mary Terese smiling.

Rosie was impressed by the principal's tactics.

"Well I can't help the way I feel. If I stay here at school I'm not going to pass any of my exams anyway. I just can't study anymore. I can't concentrate in class. I don't want to do anything anymore."

"Rosie you're giving up a lot for the sake of a boy."

"I know sister, but you wouldn't understand what if feels like" said Rosie, who was too emotional to be tactful.

"Why Rosie, because I'm a nun?" replied St Mary Terese, who was not offended in the least by Rosie's comment. She was used to people making assumptions about her lifestyle; young people in particular, assumed that because she wore a habit, she was devoid of all feelings. "You know I do remember what it feels like to be in love Rosie and I still say that there are more important things in life." Rosie was a bit shocked at the thought of Sr Mary Terese being with a man but she managed to ask,
"Like what?"
"Like getting a good job and maybe being something more than a girlfriend or wife: being a person in your own right".
"But why can't I do all that and still be with him?" asked Rosie.
"Well maybe you can Rosie, if you stay on at school and do you're exams you don't have to go to university right away. You could take a year out and go to America then."

Part of Rosie knew what Sr Mary Terese was saying made sense; the other part of her revolted inwardly at the suggestion that she wait for a whole year before seeing Jim again. She really believed that she would die if she had to wait that long.
"I can't do it Sister" she muttered finally. "I really think I'll crack up if I have to stay here."
"What if I agree that you leave school for a couple of months? You could work until Christmas and if you are still set on going to America and your parents agree then off you go; but if you change your mind you could come back to school after Christmas. I still think you could manage to pass your 'A' levels if you tried."

Rosie thought about this. She was surprised at how understanding the principal was being. Perhaps she was not just a nun. Perhaps she did have some common sense.

"That sounds like a good idea sister" she said beginning to smile.

"Will you talk to my mum and dad?"

"I can only advise them Rosie, the ultimate decision is theirs to make."

"I know sister, but they'll listen to you" said Rosie.

Sr Mary Terese recognised that there was little point in forcing Rosie to stay at school under duress. She could not afford another incident like the one just played out in Miss Kelly's class. Such behaviour was unacceptable, and if Rosie was to get away with it others would follow. If Rosie left school now it would dispense with any further need to take action. Hopefully the other pupils would assume that Rosie had been suspended and the proper message would be provided to everyone in the school. Teachers would feel supported and pupils would recognise that they could not say the 'F' word in class and get away with it. Sister Mary Terese felt satisfied with the way the situation had been handled. All she needed to do now was to talk to Rosie's parents and convince them of the need to remove Rosie from school for the time being.

Chapter Ten

It was the middle of October, and Rosie was in good spirits. She had been working full time in Morrellie's for a fortnight now and she loved it. Her mother and father were deeply disappointed in her for leaving school but had finally come around to the idea when Sister Mary Terese pointed out that Rosie was heading for expulsion if her behaviour deteriorated any further. This way there was at least a chance that Rosie could resume her studies if, or when, she finally came to her senses.

Mr and Mrs Maguire were both united in their condemnation of Rosie's plan to go to America in January. They hoped that Rosie would give up on the idea and return to school. Rosie, however, grew more determined and excited by the prospect every day. She wrote back to Jim and advised him of her intentions, the incident in school and the fact that she was now working full time. He telephoned her as soon as he received her letter and they spoke for the first time since August. Jim was openly delighted by the prospect of seeing Rosie again but was shocked by her dramatic departure from school and by the obvious annoyance she was causing her parents. He expressed some concern, and even guilt, at being the cause of her difficulties at home. Rosie reassured him that she could not bear to go to school anymore and that she couldn't wait to go to New York.

Although he longed to see Rosie again, Jim started to feel anxious about the idea of living with her. *What if they couldn't get along? What if she started nagging him? What if she expected marriage and babies?* Jim was only just starting to enjoy himself in New York. He had landed a good job and had gained the respect and friendship of his fellow workers. He was really starting to enjoy the social life in Queens. The apartment he was now sharing with Michael (or Mouse as his friends called him) would be his when Mouse returned to Ireland. Jim had made some effort with the decoration of his new place of abode. He was handy with a paint brush and he had painted the drab interior in pale neutral shades which made the place look bigger and brighter. It was very much in need of a *woman's touch* to finish it off, but Jim was pleased with the overall effect.

Mouses's plans to return to Ireland were coming together. He was determined to be in Ireland for the New Year. He was working hard and doing a lot of overtime at the bar. Jim did not see much of him and this suited both men. They were like ships passing in the night. Jim went to work early in the morning and was home by 6pm. Most days Mouse slept late and went to work in the afternoon. On his one day off, he stayed in bed all day. Jim had the weekends in the apartment to himself. He enjoyed this. He would get up early, make himself breakfast and then leave to go sight seeing. By the end of October, he had seen all there was to see in Manhattan and was spending more time in exploring the other boroughs. Every Sunday he had dinner with Mary and Stan at their place. They all enjoyed this. Jim had grown close to the couple. Stan and he enjoyed the occasional night out together, bowling or playing pool at their local.

As Christmas time approached, Jim began to feel homesick. He missed Rosie all the time, but this homesickness was different. Sometimes it was the smallest thing that would trigger it. He would see a programme on TV that would remind him of Ireland or smell a familiar scent that triggered a memory of his mother. The smell of burnt toast or tea brewing on the stove could send him reeling. The odour of freshly baked bread was particularly emotive to him. Sometimes he would wander down to the bakery on Queens Boulevard on a Saturday morning just to indulge this sensation. He would picture his mother baking soda bread on the griddle at home, and his father hovering around waiting to get the first slice while it was still hot. They didn't have soda bread in New York.

Apparently they could build the biggest skyscraper in the world but they couldn't make soda bread. Jim realised that this would be the first Christmas in his life that he had spent away from his family. Mary and Stan had invited him to spend Christmas day with Stan's family. He was not looking forward to it. Stan's parents were nice people but they talked too much and asked too many questions. Jim was anxious about spending the whole day with them.

Back home, Christmas morning was always spent on the shores of Lough Neagh shooting with his fathers and brothers, while his mother prepared dinner. After 10 o'clock mass the family would sit down to a breakfast of bacon and eggs before the men would disappear off down the fields with the dogs to enjoy a long walk around Lough Tully. Mrs O'Loan used this time to visit neighbours and friends before returning to the house to make the final preparations for dinner. The men always cleaned up afterwards with military precision. Jim's father gave directions but did little else. His mother relaxed in the living room watching the Christmas film on TV. Usually in the evening, the entire family, including Mrs O'Loan, played cards. Jim's nieces and nephew watched the adults play and the house was full of laughter mixed with the squeals of the children.

When Christmas day arrived Jim dressed in his best clothes and went to Mass at the Catholic Church in Jackson Heights. He was impressed with the service. The priest talked about love for your fellow man and prayed for peace in the world and an end to the violence in Ireland. Jim thought this was quite strange, given the level of crime in New York. He realised that he had somehow become desensitised to the violence in his own country. Providing it did not touch him personally he barely flinched when he listened to the news. He realised that a generation of young people had grown up feeling the same way: inert and powerless to change things, almost accepting of the situation their country was in. Being removed from it, he was now able to view the chaos at home through more objective eyes. It still stunk. After Mass, Jim made his way to Mary and Stan's apartment. They were delighted to see him and Jim felt instantly relaxed. Perhaps it wouldn't be such a chore to spend a whole day with them and Stan's family.

Back home in Ireland, the O'Loan family were enjoying the annual card came around the kitchen table. Everyone, bar Sean, was laughing and enjoying a drink. He alone felt removed from the festivities. He was thinking about Jim and inevitably his thoughts turned to Rosie. He had heard on the grapevine of her intentions to go to New York. He was worried. Rosie was an accident waiting to happen. Sean remembered the look on her face when he had last spoken to her in August. He remembered the pain in her eyes and the look she gave him before she got out of his car. He should have known then that Rosie would be back causing trouble. Try as he might though, Sean could not quite identify what it was about Rosie that annoyed him so. He just felt unnerved whenever he thought about her. She made him feel guilty and angry at the same time.

At that moment Rosie was thinking about Jim. She had received a huge bunch of red roses via *Interflora* on Christmas eve with a card that read simply 'Love Jim'. She had never received flowers from *Interflora* before. Her sisters and mother had been suitably impressed. Rosie squealed with delight when they arrived and displayed the bouquet on the table in the hall so everyone could see them as soon as they entered the house. Rosie also telephoned Ellie to tell her and Ellie had also been impressed. She and Rosie did not see as much of each other now that Rosie was working, but they still went out every Saturday night together and took turns to stay in each other's house afterwards.

Despite missing Jim all the time, Rosie managed to remain fairly up beat. Her sadness was tempered by her excitement about going to New York in the New Year. Her birthday was on the 2 January and she would be eighteen. Rosie had saved more than enough money for the plane ticket and she intended to book her flight after the Christmas holidays. Everything was coming together.

By Christmas time Ellie had ceased trying to talk Rosie into going back to school and had accepted her inevitable departure to the States with some grace. She wanted Rosie to be happy but she knew she would miss her. She could not help feeling a bit hurt by Rosie's apparent joy at the prospect of leaving her behind in Ireland. Ellie definitely did not get the whole *being in love* thing. From where she sat it, appeared that being in love was more of a curse than a pleasure. She too wanted to leave Ireland. In Ellie's case however, she was in search of a career and travel and fun. She did not want to leave just to shack up with a fella: and a local fella at that. She still thought Rosie was an idiot but she had to admire her determination.

It was about 8 o'clock on Christmas night when Rosie, Kate and Ellie entered the social club at Tullycross. Ann had given them a lift down the road but had refused to come in with them saying she wanted to watch the film on TV. The girls looked around for a good seat. There were already several groups of people out enjoying a Christmas night drink. Rosie headed straight for the bar and, being the only one with any money, she purchased three glasses of cider. Kate and Ellie had found a seat in the corner where they could see everyone coming in but were not instantly noticeable themselves. This suited them as, apart from Ellie, they were underage and did not wish to attract undue notice.

As the girls sipped their cider they watched the people enter the club and commented on the various Christmas outfits. Most of the men were wearing new jumpers and the girls took great delight in making fun of them.

"I swear I'll kill myself before I ever buy a man a woolly jumper" said Ellie.

"It's so twee!" agreed Rosie.

"I wish I had a man to buy a jumper for" said Kate wistfully.

"You could get any man you want Kate, I don't know why you don't have a boyfriend" said Ellie. She was genuinely surprised at Kate's comment.

"It doesn't look good for the rest of us if you can't get a fella" continued Ellie, who was growing increasingly despondent at the quality of jumpers on offer.

"Well, no one ever asks me out" sighed Kate.

"That's 'cause you're TOO good looking" commented Rosie, who was trying hard not to sound smug, given the fact that she had her Jim.

"That's not true, Rosie" said Kate quietly, "I think I'm just not that attractive to the opposite sex."

"Kate, Rosie's right, you're gorgeous" said Ellie, "it's just that men haven't the balls to ask you out. Rosie only gets asked out because she's such a slapper!"

"You bitch" snapped Rosie, "my heart belongs to one man and one man only."

"It's not you're heart they're interested in" laughed Ellie.

Rosie could not help but laugh too. Ellie had resorted to sarcasm because she knew that Rosie was leaving soon and she had been unable to persuade her to stay. This was as near to a declaration of friendship that Ellie was likely to make. Rosie felt suddenly very scared and wished that she could take Ellie with her to New York. She did not want to lose her as a friend. For the first time Rosie felt worried about going to America. What if Jim did turn out to be a completely hateful? She would be stuck in New York on her own with no friends to turn too. She'd have to phone home and admit that she'd made a mistake. How humiliating would that be?

As the girls continued to sip their drinks and chat about men, the door of the club opened and in walked Sean O'Loan. He had left his family playing cards and driven down to the club to have a quiet drink. He needed space. The noise in the house was irritating. Nieces and nephews were all right for a while, but after several hours they had started to grate on Sean's nerves. He needed a pint. Sean ordered a drink and turned to look around the bar to see if there was anyone he knew. He nodded 'hello' to several men in turn and said 'Happy Christmas' to their wives or girlfriends. Finally his gaze fell upon Rosie, Kate and Ellie. *Oh crap!* he thought, *just what I needed.* Sean nodded at the girls and then turned back quickly to the bar to retrieve his pint. He considered what he should do now. Should he leave? Perhaps he could finish his pint quickly and sneak out without having to speak to them. No, Kate would consider it rude and, while he couldn't bear to speak to Rosie, he did not want to offend Kate. Slowly Sean made his way towards the table where the girls were sitting. His eyes met Rosie's first. She was smiling smugly at him. Sean wished them all merry Christmas and asked if they had had a nice day. Ellie and Kate both responded in the affirmative. Rosie remained silent. Kate then asked how Sean's day had gone and how his family were.'

"Grand" he replied. Out of the blue, Rosie asked if he had heard from Jim lately. Sean said that his mother had a Christmas card and letter last week, and that he was due to phone home this evening.

"I'm going out to New York myself in the New Year" said Rosie, "if you have anything for Jim I'd be pleased to take it with me."

"I'll be sure and tell my ma that Rosie, it's very kind of you to offer" he said, looking Rosie square in the eye. He did not fail to note the expression on her face. She was still angry with him.

"No problem Sean!" she said, smiling sarcastically.

The tension between them was making Kate and Ellie uncomfortable. Kate could not stand it,

"Excuse me I need to go to the toilet" she said, and grabbing her bag she left the table. Ellie too wanted to leave,

"I'm going to the bar" she said. "Will you take a drink Sean?"

"No thank you Ellie, I'm driving!" Ellie nodded and also left the table taking Rosie's purse with her. Sean looked at Rosie. She held his stare. She was a defiant little person.

"You're still angry with me Rosie" he said,

"I was . . . but I'm not now" she lied.

"I wish we could be friends Rosie" he said simply. Rosie was surprised by his statement. She could not remember exactly why she was angry with him. Now that she was soon to be reunited with Jim she no longer felt the grief of separation. She was not really a vindictive person and she found it difficult to sustain anger.

"I'd like that" she said, "no point in crying over spilt milk." Sean smiled. He looked handsome when he did. His face relaxed and his eyes twinkled.

"Good! Now that's settled who's buying the drink?" he asked, sitting down beside Rosie and making himself comfortable. By the time Ellie and Kate returned to the table Rosie and Sean were talking and laughing warmly together. The two girls looked at each other in disbelief. Ellie was convinced Rosie had finally lost the plot. She was sitting with the enemy and appeared to be enjoying herself. "I see you two have made it up at last!" she said, squeezing past Rosie and sitting down opposite Sean.

"Yeah, Rosie can't live without me you see!" replied Sean looking first at Rosie and then over at Ellie. Rosie laughed out loud.

"What could I do, he looked so pathetic that I had to forgive him!"

"I see you're still as delusional as ever Rosie. Are you sure you're taking your medication the way the doctor prescribed it. You know you shouldn't take it all at once."

"Very funny smart ass!" snapped Rosie.

Ellie and Kate enjoyed seeing Sean tease Rosie. She was so easily wound up and Sean had a great way with the one liners.

As the evening progressed, several others joined the company. Young men who would not normally have had the courage to approach Kate were spurred on by the fact that Sean was sitting at the table. They used his presence as an introduction and were soon asked to sit down and join the company. Kate's usual shyness was masked considerably by the presence of Rosie and Ellie and she soon found herself talking freely to a young man called Michael, who was a work mate of Sean's. Kate knew Michael Green to see but had never spoken to him before. He was fair haired and blue eyed and over six feet tall. He was smitten by Kate almost as soon as Sean introduced them and as the evening progressed it was obvious to everyone at the table that Kate had made a conquest.

Ellie was also enjoying the craic at the table but had not met anyone whom she found particularly attractive. Ellie's views on what constituted an attractive man were not conventional. She regarded most Northern Irish men as insular, unsophisticated and lacking in style. She longed to meet a man with a different accent. She quite fancied the idea of marrying a foreigner and living far away from rainy Ireland. Unfortunately, to the outside world, Northern Ireland presented itself as such an unattractive place to live that it was rare indeed to meet anyone who was not of either Celtic or Anglo descent, or both. As she looked around the bar Ellie imagined what it would be like if Northern Ireland were to be invaded by a foreign nation who knew how to dance and didn't wear jumpers. *Come back Vikings, all is forgiven!* she mused to herself.

At the end of the evening, Sean offered the girls a lift home. They were glad not to have to walk as it was a chilly night and, as usual, Rosie had left her coat in the house. Rosie automatically jumped into the front seat of Sean's car. She thought it strange how comfortable she now felt with him when only hours before she could not think of him without getting angry. Sean continued the conversation in the car on the way home, periodically turning to Rosie to check her responses to his constant jibes and teasing. Rosie held her own. She had noticed how well read Sean was on subjects that also interested her. He had talked about movies and music and made reference to historical events and expressed opinions that enthralled Rosie. She had grown increasingly impressed by his overall wit and by the time they arrived at the Maguire's front door Rosie felt that she did not want to say good night. She did not know when she would see Sean again. Automatically she asked if he wished to come in for a cup of tea. As it was only just after 11 o'clock, and he was on holiday, Sean found himself saying yes. For some reason he did not wish to say good night. Ellie and Kate got out of the back seat of the car followed by Rosie and Sean. Rosie immediately went to check if her mother and father were in bed and to tell them she was home,

"Sean O'Loan gave us a lift up the road Ma, and we're just making him a cup of tea" she said, in response to her mother's query about how the girls had gotten home.

"OK" replied Mrs Maguire, "but keep the noise down, the youngsters are asleep."

"Righto Ma!" replied Rosie.

"Night Night" Kate whispered to her mother through the open bedroom door,

"Good night Mrs Maguire" added Ellie,

"Good night girls," Mrs Maguire replied, adding "good night Mr O'Loan." Sean did not know whether or not to answer. He eventually stammered,

"Good night Mrs Maguire" and hurried into the kitchen behind Ellie and Kate who were already preparing tea and toast for supper. Rosie followed behind and started to laugh as soon as the kitchen door was closed. Sean smiled. He thought it was sweet that Mrs Maguire had spoken to him from the depths of her bedroom and that she had managed to imply so much with the simple phrase 'goodnight'. She was warning him, not to overstay his welcome, nor to take advantage of her hospitality (or her daughters). Sean thought momentarily what it would be like to take advantage of Rosie. She was gorgeous; warm and alive and full of youth and life. She was still laughing at him and her eyes sparkled as they mocked him. For a moment he felt a deep longing to hold her. The longing passed when Rosie spoke to him,

"Do you want some cheese and toast Sean?" she asked, unaware of the feelings she was stirring inside him. The thought of food restored his equilibrium and Sean nodded eagerly,

"I'm starving" he replied.

"Actually there's plenty of turkey and ham left over. Let's have some of that!" said Kate.

As the four young people munched on turkey and ham sandwiches, they talked of the evenings events.

"I think you have smitten young Michael, Kate" said Sean. Kate blushed and said.

"He's alright I suppose."

"Did he get your number? asked Ellie, keen to find out if Kate would be seeing him again.

"No" she replied, pausing for a moment before adding, "but he said he would call and take me out tomorrow for a drive."

"Kate has a boyfriend" rhymed Ellie. Kate blushed again, obviously enjoying the ribbing and flushed with the excitement of a first romantic encounter. She had enjoyed talking to Michael. She felt comfortable with his simple talk about his work and family. They had much in common. She was generally a warm-hearted person and, beneath her composed exterior, Kate Maguire's heart beat as wildly as her sister Rosie's. Kate was known for having a short temper and reacted to injustice as passionately as any of her sisters. Any signs of a perceived threat to her dignity or her rights resulted in Kate snapping like a viper provoked. Luckily, she did not mind being teased about Michael. Somehow it felt good.

When the supper was finished, Rosie and Kate cleared the dishes into the sink and began the washing up. Sean offered to help, but Ellie interrupted him pointing out that Rosie was,

". . . only tidying up because you're here. You know she'd usually leave them lying on the table for me to do!"

"I would not!" Rosie snapped indignantly. "I do most of the cleaning in this house."

"That's 'cause you do most of the messing" said Kate. Sean listened as the girls continued to tease each other, watching Rosie's face as she feigned anger then laughed. Again he felt the desire to hold her. Had they been alone he probably would have tried. He was strangely glad that Kate and Ellie were there. They stopped him from doing something which he knew he would regret. Rosie was not interested in him in that way. She was in love with his younger brother and, for all he knew, Jim was in love with her. He decided to leave. Standing up he lifted his coat from the back of his chair saying,

"Well I better be going. Thanks for the supper girls."

"Thank you for the lift" said Kate. Ellie too thanked him for the lift home. She and Kate were both tired and wanted to go to bed. Rosie wanted a cigarette.

"I'll let you out Sean" she said, grabbing her bag and heading for the door. Sean followed her, saying a final good night to Kate and Ellie.

Rosie closed the front door behind her, as she and Sean stepped into the cold night air. Sean stared at her wondering why she had come outside with him. Just as he was beginning to hope that she too had wanted to be alone with him, Rosie announced that she was 'choking for a cigarette'. Sean was disappointed,
"Oh," he said, pausing for a moment to regain his status quo, "I thought you were following me outside to seduce me Rosie."
"You wish!" she laughed. *Yes, I kinda do,* thought Sean. Rosie began to shiver.
"You'll catch your death Rosie Maguire" said Sean, putting his coat around her as if she was a small child, "not to mention lung cancer" he added, as Rosie fumbled in her hand bag for her cigarettes.
"Who are you, my mother?" she retorted suddenly forgetting about her cigarettes and looking up into his face. He was staring at her. Rosie met his gaze defiantly,
"What you looking at?" she asked nervously.
"I'm looking at you Rosie" Sean replied calmly. Rosie was transfixed. Why did he make her feel so uncomfortable? She dropped her gaze and was about to turn away when Sean reached out his hand and touched her chin, gently guiding her face back towards his. He then bent down and kissed her: on the forehead.
"Good night Rosie" he said, and walked towards his car without glancing back. Rosie was struck dumb. It was only when Sean had driven away from the house that she realised

she was still wearing his coat. Instinctively she thrust her arms into the sleeves and drew the coat tightly around her, hugging the leather closer to her body. She could smell his aftershave and also his own scent. It warmed her insides.

"Weirdo!" she announced to the world in general and then lit up a cigarette.

Chapter Eleven

It was the 2 January 1985 when Rosie turned 18. She received the usual cards and small presents from her sisters. Generally the boys were exempt from giving birthday presents to the family (apart from Mrs Maguire). Nobody knew why. That was just always the way it had been. Rosie's parents presented her with a silver bracelet with her named engraved on it,

"It's so you don't forget who you are Rosie" said her father.

"I never will" she replied, first hugging and kissing her father, then her mother.

"You know Rosie you can always come home if things don't work out in New York" said Mrs Maguire as she held Rosie in her arms. Rosie knew that her mother was worried about her. Mrs Maguire had accepted the fact that Rosie was going, but she had grave misgivings about it. She could not shake the sense of foreboding she felt every time she thought of her daughter crossing the Atlantic and beginning a new life in a place like New York. She figured no good could possibly come of it, but she was wise enough to know that no good could come from any attempt to stand between Rosie and her *destiny*. "Sure I'll be back in no time at all" said Rosie, attempting to reassure her parents. They were not convinced. Mrs Maguire remembered the living wakes that were held when local people decided to emigrate to the States in the 40s and 50s. Family and friends gathered and held parties to honour the soon to be *departed*. The expectation was that it would be many, many years before they would be able to visit home again. While Mrs Maguire knew the world was now a smaller place, she could not shake the fear she felt deep down that she would not see Rosie again for a long time.

For her part, Rosie was in excellent spirits. She had finished work on Christmas Eve and had been given an extra bonus payment in her wages. The staff at Morrellie's had also presented her with a gift of $100 for her American trip and had wished her well. Tony Morrellie was genuinely upset to see her go. He gave Rosie a silver, St Christopher Medal. Rosie was deeply touched by the kindness of her fellow workers and her boss. she cried when she was saying goodbye. Now she could not contain her joy at the prospect of going to New York to be with Jim. She had given little thought to the impact on her family and friends of her departure but, as the time drew nearer for her to go, Rosie began to feel nervous. On 6 January she was sitting in her bedroom with Ellie. As she packed her bags and made final preparations for her trip (she was due to fly out on the 8 January) she began to doubt her decision to leave,

"Do you think I'm not wise Ellie?" she queried, hoping for some reassurance from her friend.

"Of course Rosie" replied Ellie, "you never where!"

"I'm serious" whined Rosie, "what if I really don't like it there?"

"Then you come home again Rosie" stated Ellie, matter-of-factly.

"But what if Jim won't come with me?"

"Then you leave him there and get on with your own life Rosie" said Ellie, who never failed to be irritated by Rosie's apparent dependence on Jim O'Loan. Ellie could not bear the thought of any one man having such a hold on her. *If that is love you can have it* she thought.

"I suppose so," muttered Rosie, not picking up on Ellie's irritation. Ellie looked at her and began to wonder just when her friend had become such a drip. She felt disloyal for thinking so, but Rosie really had lost all of her individuality and spontaneity since she had fallen in love with Jim,

"For the life of me Rosie I don't know why you just don't marry the guy and have done with it" she sighed. For Ellie the thought of being married at eighteen was about as appealing as beginning a life sentence in Long Kesh.

"Oh, wouldn't that be wonderful if he just proposed when I got there and we got married right away?" said Rosie, sighing to herself.

"Oh boke Rosie!" Ellie stated, putting two fingers into her mouth and pretending to retch.

"What do you mean Ellie? Don't you want to get married and have children?" asked Rosie, who could think of nothing finer.

"Frankly Rosie, I'd rather chew me own foot off" snapped Ellie, who was quickly tiring of the conversation.

"You have no heart Ellie" said Rosie, feeling suddenly very sorry for Ellie and extremely smug about herself.

"And you have lost whatever brains you ever had" retorted Ellie "along with your personality and the last of your sanity."

139

"Well you can't expect me to live, while my true love is a million miles away."

"Shows you what you know Rosie, New York is five thousand miles away"

"You know what I mean" retorted Rosie.

"Don't you go getting all snippy with me Rosie Maguire just because you're having doubts about flying half way round the world to be with a young lad."

"I am not having doubts!" said Rosie angrily. "I love Jim and he loves me so why shouldn't we be together?"

"I'll tell you why Rosie, because you are becoming a complete bore. All you ever think or talk about is Jim O'Loan, and I'm sick of it. You never once thought about how I might feel about you going away or about the plans we had made. Men are all well and good Rosie but it's your friends you'll need when Jim O'Loan gets bored with you and finds himself another girl."

"Ooh" seethed Rosie, "you complete bitch Ellie McKeown. You're just jealous 'cause you haven't got anyone and you're going to die an old maid!"

"Well you're full of mad dog shite Rosie Maguire and I hope you rot in New York with your stupid boyfriend in your stupid love nest."

"Well I hate you too!" shouted Rosie, before bursting into tears. Ellie felt bad.

"I hate you more" she said quietly.

"I hate you the most" sniffed Rosie through her tears.

"Stop crying you fat cow" muttered Ellie, beginning to sniff too.

"You stop!"

"I'm not crying!" sniffed Ellie.

"I'm going to miss you ya' ol'bitch!" muttered Rosie.

"What was that?" asked Ellie,

"Nothing!"

"Something about missing me I think you said." Ellie was smiling now, and Rosie could not help smiling too.

"I think I WILL miss you."

"Personally I'm looking forward to the break from you Rosie Maguire, but if you wish you may write to me occasionally and I might even reply."

"You are too kind Ellie".

"Well one must indulge the lower classes when one can" replied Ellie, feigning an aristocratic accent and nodding graciously at Rosie as if she was royalty.

"You big eejit Ellie. I love you" said Rosie, and gave Ellie a hug. Ellie smiled,

"I love you too, idiot!"

Five thousand miles away Jim O'Loan was also making final preparations. The imminent arrival of Rosie was all he could think about. He had tidied the apartment and purchased new soft furnishings from Bloomingdale's. The apartment looked good. His main dilemma concerned the sleeping arrangements. Mouse had left for Ireland on the day before Christmas Eve, and his room was free. Jim could not, however, imagine Rosie being under the same roof as himself and sleeping in another room, but he was worried that she might be offended if he assumed that they were to sleep together. Then again, he did not want her to think that he was gay if he made up the spare room. He finally decided that he would prepare the spare room for her coming, but also make his own room look extremely inviting and hope that Rosie would take the hint.

When he had cleaned all that there was to clean and had redecorated the spare room Jim felt quite pleased with the overall effect. The apartment was bright and modern but with a homely feel to it. He knew Rosie would be pleased. It was the 6 January and he still had two days left to wait for Rosie's arrival. Jim was out of his mind with excitement. He felt as he used to when he was a child in the days coming up to Christmas. He remembered not being able to sleep properly on Christmas Eve because he was so excited about his presents. He also remembered that Christmas day itself never quite measured up to how he had imagined it would be. Very often by Boxing day he was left feeling totally under whelmed as if something had been taken from him but he wasn't sure what. Definitely the anticipation of Christmas was by far the best part. Jim wondered if he would feel the same when Rosie finally did arrive. He then wondered if Rosie was having the same doubts. He had spoken to her on her birthday and again yesterday to confirm final arrangements and she sounded so excited he was worried that she would ultimately be disappointed with him or with New York and not want to stay. He had arranged for a friend, Gerry, to drive him to JFK to collect Rosie. He now wished he had chosen to go alone. He wanted to greet her with flowers and to make their reunion as romantic as possible. He could not do that with his friend Gerry hanging about. Gerry was a tough, older man from the Falls Road in Belfast. He would not approve off public displays of affection and he would rib Jim for ages if he brought flowers for Rosie.

When the day finally dawned and Rosie Maguire landed in New York, Jim spotted her coming thought the terminal and forgot all his previous anxieties. Rushing forward, ignoring Gerry's pleas for restraint, he swept Rosie off her feet and into the air before she had time to say his name. He held her tightly for several minutes before covering her face and mouth in kisses. Rosie was overwhelmed, not least with embarrassment. She had spotted the disapproving look on Gerry's face and, after managing to steady herself, she nodded in his direction indicating to Jim to introduce her to his friend. Gerry walked forward when Jim called him and said 'hello' to Rosie. She recognised the accent and smiled as she commented on how unexpected the Belfast accent sounded. She had been expecting to meet her first New Yorker. Gerry laughed, saying that there were more Irish people in New York than there were back home. Jim nodded in agreement. As they walked towards Gerry's car, Rosie continued her conversation with Gerry while Jim wheeled her luggage in the trolley. He was able to take time to look at her now as she chatted animatedly to her new acquaintance. He thought she had grown older somehow since he last saw her. Her hair was longer and she'd had it permed. She was also wearing make-up and high heels. Rosie thought she looked very sophisticated. Jim thought she looked a bit cheap. He was old-fashioned in his views about women and how they should look and behave. He was not sure if he liked Rosie's new look but he was not overly concerned. He would talk to her about it later. Meantime, Rosie was trying her best to sound interested in whatever Gerry said, but all she really wanted was to be alone with Jim and to continue with the kissing and hugging. She was too well-mannered to ignore Gerry however, so she kept the conversation going all the way back to Jackson Heights and to Jim's apartment.

When they arrived at the apartment, Gerry helped Jim carry Rosie's luggage upstairs but he refused to stay for a coffee, saying that he would catch Jim later for 'a pint'. Rosie was relieved when he left but, as she turned to look at Jim, alone for the first time, she suddenly became extremely shy and awkward and was unsure how to behave. Jim made the first move reaching out to her and drawing her close to him. They kissed then for a very long time until any anxiety on either part faded into oblivion. As Jim's hands began to wander over her body and his kisses became more urgent, Rosie realised suddenly that she was an adult; she was alone and she could do whatever she wanted. She felt completely alive and exhilarated. She had not one sensible thought in her head and every nerve in her body was pulsating with passion for Jim. Before long, the young couple managed to stumble through the open door of Jim's bedroom and onto the bed. From that moment on, the sleeping arrangements were settled. Rosie had plucked up the courage to go and see her GP long before she left for the states and he had given her the pill. She was not particularly happy about taking it but she was wise enough to know that she could not rely on Jim to take precautions against pregnancy. In the event Jim, had not even asked her about contraception. He was overcome with passion and was too embarrassed to talk about such things with a girl. Like many Irish men, Jim was fine with having sex but was incapable of talking about it or any possible consequences.

The first few days and weeks in New York flew by for Rosie. She was having the time of her life. By the end of the second week, she had done all of the major tourist attractions in Manhattan and was quite confident travelling alone on the subway system. Before coming to New York, Rosie had read every book in the local library about the city and the surrounding boroughs. She had also purchased a very expensive guide book which she read from cover to cover on the plane on the flight over from Ireland. As Jim was working during the day, he was not able to accompany Rosie on her weekday trips. They had breakfast together every morning before Jim left for work. Then Rosie would do some housework before showering and getting herself ready to spend the day sightseeing (and job hunting of course). She was usually back by 4 o'clock in the afternoon and she would then start to make dinner for Jim who was generally home before six.

On their first weekend together, Jim took Rosie to Liberty Island, Ellis Island and on the Staten Island Ferry. It was bitterly cold on the boat but Rosie enjoyed every minute. She was able to provide Jim with a running commentary on the history of just about everything they saw. She would have made an excellent tour guide and Jim was amazed at how she remembered all that information. Rosie was secretly amazed at how little Jim knew. Rosie believed it was her duty to enlighten him. Jim believed Rosie talked too much.

On the second weekend she was there, Jim took Rosie to Central Park. It had snowed heavily the night before, and the pond near the 5thAvenue entrance was frozen over. Rosie and Jim stood on the little humped back bridge and watched people skating. It was very pretty. Jim asked if she wanted to take a ride around the park in a horse drawn carriage. Initially Rosie thought this would be very romantic but when they approached the horses the smell of manure and horse repulsed Rosie and she changed her mind about the ride. Somehow when she got close to horses, the romance always seemed to fade. She thought horses looked magnificent on television and she longed to be able to gallop over the hills with her hair blowing in the wind: a fine steed between her legs. The truth was that Rosie did not actually like horses. They were one of the few things in the world that she had the wit to be scared of. They were big, unpredictable and smelly. Rosie declined Jim's offer but asked him to take her to the Metropolitan Museum instead.

"You were there last week Rosie" Jim pointed out. He was not keen on museums as he thought they were all very boring and filled with 'old crap'.

"I know but I only got to see a wee bit of it 'cause I spent all my time in the European art section. I didn't get to see the half what I wanted to," she replied, beginning to hop about from one foot to another, getting ready to whine if Jim didn't want to go.

"I'd rather go on the horse and carriage ride . . ." Jim protested trying to think quickly of ways to avoid the museum, "it's more romantic" he added hastily.

"There is nothing romantic about freezing your backside off in an open carriage with a horse's arse looking straight at you," quipped Rosie.

"We could cuddle under the blanket" suggested Jim. Rosie sighed deeply. She was beginning to feel all Jim ever wanted to do was have sex with her or have pre sex groping.

"Jim I'd like to see the museum because it has stuff in it that I may never get to see again. I had to travel from Europe to America to see paintings by European masters like Rembrandt and Monet and that Spanish guy. Do you know they have a hall full of Ancient Greek statues and one of Roman stuff and I didn't even get to see the mummies yet." Jim's eye lit up at the thought of the Egyptian mummies. This was something he could relate to,

"OK" he said, "we'll go to the museum to see a bunch of dead fellas wrapped in sheets, as long as I don't have to look at crappy paintings of flowers and women in big dresses." Rosie laughed. She had come very near to having her first New York argument with Jim and it had made her feel very insecure. Looking at him now, she thought he looked very handsome and, for a lad of twenty, he looked remarkably together and in control. She liked that about him. She also liked how his ass looked in jeans. Once again Rosie's cup was spilling over and she smiled happily to herself as those quiet nagging doubts about her relationship with Jim grew silent once more.

The following week Rosie was lucky enough to get a job working in a café/ice cream parlour in Queens. She had walked past Ricardo's several times on her way to catch the train into Manhattan, and thought it looked interesting. There was no neon shamrock on the outside. For Rosie this was a plus. The only places that Jim ever seemed to want to frequent were Irish bars. This did not make sense to Rosie. She much preferred meeting native New Yorkers and other foreigners than any one from back home. After all, she had been meeting Irish people all her life and now she could meet people from all over the world. Another huge plus was the fact that Ricardo's sold home made ice cream. Rosie considered herself to be a connoisseur. One afternoon, on her return from Manhattan, she was unable to resist the draw of the magical substance. It had been a particularly hard days sightseeing which had included the Guggenheim and the Frick museums. Rosie's feet where tired and she was graving sugar. As she approached the ice cream parlour the eponymous owner appeared and smiled at her. He indicated to her to come into his café and sample his 'marvellous cuisine'. Rosie did not have to be asked twice. She walked in and, after a speed read of the dessert menu, she ordered a banana split and a cup of coffee. Ricardo laughed at the combination, but proceeded to make her the largest banana split she had ever seen.

Ricardo was third generation Italian descent. He spoke with a very broad Queens accent and he was a very big man. Ricardo had obviously been handsome in his younger days. He behaved as if he still was: flirting outrageously with all the female staff who worked for him. His little wife, Cecelia, scolded him constantly, fearing always that her big, handsome husband would run off with one of the many females he came in contact with. She still considered him to be a fine catch after forty years of marriage and was as jealous as she had been when she first started dating him as a sixteen year old girl.

When Rosie finished eating, Ricardo could not help but comment on her most enthusiastic appreciation of his fine ice cream. He had enjoyed watching her consume the dish with so much obvious pleasure. Rosie was always in her happiest place when she was eating but, when presented with such a gift to the overall senses as that magnificent banana split, she was practically euphoric. Ricardo recognised her as a great proficient in the appreciation of food and was immediately drawn to her. They chatted while Rosie sipped her coffee and before long it was established that Ricardo was short on staff; Rosie needed a job and, therefore, it made sense that Rosie would start work the following day on a trial basis.

Rosie could not wait to tell Jim her news that evening when he got home from work. She made a big effort with dinner, cooking a lovely beef casserole with potatoes and vegetables, and of course ice cream from Ricardo's for dessert. Jim was just complimenting her on dinner when she told him the news. He was extremely happy. Jim was starting to feel the strain of paying the rent on the apartment alone. They would easily be able to manage now if Rosie was working and contributing to the overall running costs of the place. Jim hugged Rosie tightly and kissed her several times before returning to his dish of ice cream. Italians really did make the best ice cream.

Chapter Twelve

Time continued to pass quickly for Rosie on her great American adventure. Back home for Ellie it was as if time had stalled. She was completely bored in school without Rosie. She was also overwhelmed with the amount of work she would have to do, if she really wanted to get the grades to go the university. Life was generally shit at that time; Ellie was starting to wonder if Rosie had been the one with the right idea when she had pissed off to the States and left it all behind.

Rosie's family were also missing her but there were fringe benefits to be enjoyed when she was away. Anne no longer had to come home at weekends to a state of chaos in her bed room. Kate no longer had to hide her clothes. Orlagh no longer had to do 'favours' for Rosie (like doing the dishes when it was Rosie's turn). Mr and Mrs Maguire too were enjoying the greater harmony in the house but, while there was less noise and less fighting when Rosie was away, there was also less laughter and everyone missed that.

Rosie was missing home too but her overall homesickness was kept at bay by the continued sense of excitement she felt with every new day. The job was going well. Everyone at Ricardo's was really nice to her. Even Cecelia warmed to her when she realised that Rosie had a steady boyfriend and would not be a rival for her husband's affections. Rosie was generally very happy: except when she was alone for any length of time. When left to her own devices Rosie tended to brood and her mood would alter dramatically, depending on the theme of her current thoughts. She would start to think 'what if' and her mind would become unsettled with her imaginary troubles. She would imagine Jim meeting another woman and falling in love and leaving her. She would imagine being alone in New York too embarrassed to return home a failure. She wondered sometimes about becoming pregnant and Jim leaving her. She would have to raise the child alone, and they would both probably starve to death; the thought of starving to death was particularly repugnant to Rosie. She imagined being in an accident and being far from home. She had no health insurance and would probably be left lying on the side of the road with no one to look after her, Jim having left her. Jim leaving her was a constant theme in Rosie's reveries. Sometimes, she thought so hard that she could feel the actual pain of his betrayal and the grief of his loss to the point where she would burst into tears. In reality Rosie enjoyed crying. It was a great release for her ebullient emotions which bubbled too near the surface at all times and which were responsible for her erratic and at times irresponsible behaviours. For example, Rosie remained a danger on the road, a problem which was magnified a thousand fold when she was in New York. The traffic was relentless and the drivers unpredictable. Back home, Rosie reasoned that any decent driver was bound to see her if she was walking across a road in front of them. In

New York Rosie slowly began to realise that drivers would drive over you, even if they did see you, their point being that they had the right of way. Rosie didn't have a point. If she saw nothing in front of her she walked on. She never bothered to look sideways or to try and see the whole picture and she never looked back.

Jim scolded Rosie often about her lack of common sense. He was shocked, for example, when he found out how far her individual journeys into Manhattan had taken Rosie. She had walked down every avenue and along most of the streets in Lower and Middle Manhattan. It was only when Rosie announced one morning that she intended to visit Harlem that Jim put his foot down and stated clearly 'not on my watch.' He had argued that she was just asking for trouble and that she was a 'crime waiting to happen'. Rosie had attempted to reason with Jim but, when he became angry, she let the subject drop comforting herself in the knowledge that he loved her and was afraid for her. In her own heart, Rosie knew that she would still go to Harlem but, maybe not for a while, and she certainly would not tell Jim about it. She didn't want him to worry.

One evening in the middle of April, not long after the Harlem debate, Jim took Rosie into Manhattan for a night on the town. Rosie was delighted. She had been all over Manhattan during the day time but it was expensive to travel into the city by taxi and the subway was not safe at night (according to Jim). Rosie only went to Manhattan in the evening if Jim was with her. After enjoying a leisurely walk through Time Square, Rosie showed Jim her favourite place in the whole of New York; it was Sardi's, off Broadway, where the stars of stage and screen would congregate after a show to eat and drink or just to be seen. Jim walked towards the door with Rosie but hesitated at the entrance. He felt that the restaurant was too exclusive for the likes of himself and Rosie. Rosie however, completely unabashed, sauntered in and walked straight up to the bar where she promptly sat down on a bar stole and began talking to the bar man 'Joe'. 'Hello Rosie' Joe replied in answer to her greeting, "are you not going to introduce me to your friend?"

"Joe, this is Jim O'Loan" Rosie stated matter-of-factly. Joe, who was originally from Algeria, spoke perfect English. He was a very tall man with a huge smile and dancing eyes that immediately said welcome. He was in his late forties at least. He smiled at Jim and said 'hello.' Jim was dumbfounded that Rosie, not only had been to Sardis without him, but was obviously was a regular. He suddenly wondered if he had been wise allowing Rosie to spend so much time alone in Manhattan, when she had first arrived.

If Rosie had known that Jim thought he had any say in where she went she would have been deeply piqued. To date they had never argued about sexism or male chauvinism but Rosie's feeling regarding women's rights were well known to anyone who truly knew her. From the age of six, when a boy in her class had told her boys were better than girls and Rosie had knocked him sideways on to his ass, Rosie had held extremely firm feminist beliefs. Her beliefs did not interfere with her romantic notions about love. Rosie believed that it was only truly as equals that two people could love each other properly. She had noticed on one or two occasions that Jim could come across as a little domineering and, of course, he did always wait for her to cook dinner even when they both had been out working all day long. On one occasion, he had even referred to her as his 'woman'. Rosie thought at the time that he was being facetious and had laughed. Jim, who did not know why Rosie laughed, had laughed also and said nothing. He did not call her his 'woman' again but, in his heart, he still considered her to be 'his'. Rosie believed that no person belonged to another person. She strongly believed that if the patriarchal system had been obliterated when humans first climbed down from the trees then the world would be a better place.

Jim said hello to Joe who then turned back to Rosie and asked what she would like to drink. Rosie asked for an *Absolute* and cranberry.

'No more strawberry daiquiris Rosie?' Joe enquired. Rosie laughed and Jim looked quizzically at them both. By way of explanation, Rosie told him that when she first visited Sardi's she had been overwhelmed with excitement because she knew the place was frequented by stars. Joe had spotted her staring around wide eyed and trembling with excitement and had asked her if she was lost. Rosie explained that she was from Ireland and had read about Sardi's and had always wanted to visit. As it was very early in the day she was not sure what to drink to mark the occasion and had asked Joe to make her a cocktail. He made her a strawberry daiquiri, which he served to her as she sat on a bar stool which Lauren Bacall had been sitting on the very night before. Since there first meeting Rosie had visited Sardi's on several occasions making sure that she called in before lunch time and only when she knew Joe was working. She would sit on *her* bar stool and chat animatedly to Joe, who told her stories about the stars who had visited Sardis. Joe knew that Rosie was underage, but in her high heels and make up she could just about pass of twenty one, and he covered himself by not actually asking her what age she was.

As Jim watched Rosie interact with Joe, he wondered if he really knew anything about her. She was talking to Joe about absolute rubbish, in Jim's opinion, but Joe seemed enthralled. Quite often Jim would switch off completely when Rosie was talking. She jumped from one subject to another and would regale him with stories about her days work including a running commentary on how she felt about absolutely everything. He nodded in places and said 'yes' and 'no' periodically but he didn't really hear her. Jim was unnerved now by the obvious interest that Joe displayed in what Rosie was saying. They had started quoting whole scenes from Monty Pythons *Life of Brian* when Jim finally interrupted and asked for a beer. He knew that Joe was not flirting with Rosie and that she was not flirting with him, but Jim still felt that Rosie was somehow betraying him. It was like she was a different person with other people. Joe automatically said,

"Coming right up", to Jim's request, but continued talking to Rosie as he poured the drink. Jim could not seem to find any natural inlet into the conversation between Joe and Rosie so he lapsed into silence.

Eventually Rosie noticed that Jim was quieter than usual and attempted to draw him into the discussion she had been having with Joe about his love of old B Movies. Rosie had named her favourite as being *The Attack of the Fifty Foot Woman*. Joe replied that, of course, it would be the favourite of such a feminist as Rosie. Jim heard the term feminist and was immediately baffled. Rosie was a feminist? "What do mean?" he asked Joe. Joe was slightly taken aback by Jim's sudden interest in the conversation, but he replied candidly while starting to laugh,

"Oh you know Rosie, always talking about women's rights and all. I think she would enjoy being fifty feet tall so she could kick some male chauvinist ass!" Jim smiled and tried to laugh too but he was confused. Rosie never spoke to him about her apparent feminist beliefs. He made a mental note to talk to her about it later. *I mean she can think what she likes* he reasoned *so long as she knew he was in charge and she didn't shave her hair off and start wearing Dr Martin boots.*

The rest of the evening was spent wandering around taking in the sights, sounds and hustle that is Broadway and Time Square. Later, back in Queens, Rosie and Joe stopped in their local Irish pub to have a night cap. As they sipped over their drinks, Jim's mind was drawn back to the earlier conversation in Sardi's and he decided to ask Rosie about her beliefs,

"What did your fella Joe mean about you being a feminist Rosie?" Jim asked, trying to sound casual. Rosie immediately became animated and launched into a well rehearsed, and often quoted, speech about how the entire history of mankind had been corrupted by the belief, historically held by men, that they are somehow better than women and ergo the boss of everybody. Rosie cited many examples of this delusional behaviour: stating that all wars and most of the misery in the world was the result of male pride, male ego, male dominance and male thinking.

"So what you are saying Rosie is that you hate men," Jim said when she finished, astounded by her passion for the subject.

"I don't hate men Jim," Rosie stated calmly, "I think they are very useful and everybody should have *at least* one, if they are that way inclined!" Rosie was clearly trying to lighten the mood, but Jim was still horror struck by the depth of her feeling and was reeling from how little he actually knew the girl he had been sleeping with for weeks now. Rosie noted the look on his face and began to panic slightly,

"Why are you so surprised Jim?" she asked, "you don't really believe that women should be subservient to men or that we shouldn't have the vote or that we belong to our nearest male relative?"

"No" replied Jim hesitantly, "but I just don't like thinking of you as some butch lesbian type." Rosie stared at him for a while and then smiled,

"Jim" she said, "I think we have both established that I am not a lesbian and, as far as being butch is concerned, I am quite willing to acknowledge that, generally speaking, men are physically stronger than women. What I don't accept is that this should automatically give men the right to oppress women or launch into war every time some other man starts acting all uppity and showing off, and I do REALLY believe that men and women are meant to compliment each other and live in harmony."

"Rosie, you are full of it!" snapped Jim. He was irritated by her condescending manner and he now realised what had been annoying him all evening. It was not that Rosie changed when she was with other people; she changed when she was with him. If they were spending time together she would talk about things that interested him, but she saved her own

157

interests to discuss with friends or even complete strangers. Rosie did not think that he was intelligent enough to get her. Jim was hurt by this, but his male pride was also stung by the thought that Rosie probably was more intelligent than he was. For her part Rosie was mystified by Jim's sudden annoyance. She had always known that she was smarter than he was but had been meticulous in her attempts to disguise the fact, knowing how fragile the male ego can be. Now she had been forced to show her hand by his outright demand to know how she felt about a subject that was not just near to her heart, but was an integral part of her being. Rosie had been a feminist long before she knew what the term meant. In her mind anyone with half a brain should be a feminist too, including men. They had now reached an impasse. Rosie could not take back what she had said nor could she obliterate Jim's new found knowledge. Jim could not stop imagining Rosie with a skin head and wearing combat gear. He could not ditch the feeling that Rosie was no longer the girl he had fallen in love with. They were both silent, Rosie enveloped in a growing sense of panic, and Jim in a fuming rage of shame and embarrassment. Neither could break the silence; Rosie, who usually found it impossible to remain quiet for any length of time, could not bring herself to speak for fear that she would add more fuel to the fire of Jim's internal seething. As they sat in silence, Jim looked at Rosie's downturned face and watched her misery. Every emotion was written across her troubled face. He saw all at once that she had never meant to hurt him. She loved him despite their obvious differences. What he had to accept was that, while he meant more to her than anything else in the world, he could never be her entire world. She needed other people. She missed her family and her sisters and her friends. She had no real female contacts in New York who she could talk to, and whenever she did talk about anything other than what interested him he could not bring himself to even listen. She, on the other hand, had listened to him whenever he talked about his job and the guys he met on the various sites he worked on. She asked pertinent questions and laughed appropriately at his anecdotes. She remembered the names of the people he mentioned. She encouraged him to go for a drink with work mates after work occasionally so that he could do 'that male bonding thing.' He had never once considered that Rosie might need to talk to other people. He had been content to think that he was all she needed. Suddenly Jim felt regret at his actions. He struggled with this feeling. *Was it guilt?* He was unfamiliar with the emotion and he was unsure what to do with it.

"I'm sorry Rosie" he said quietly. She slowly lifted her head and he saw the tears brimming beneath her half shut eyelids. "Really?" she asked, a look of genuine disbelief on her face. "You sound surprised" he said.

"I'm not sure what else to say?" Rosie sniffed, "I mean, are you saying you're sorry we met, you're sorry it's over, you're sorry we had a fight? . . . . you're sorry for being a dick? What?" Jim flinched at the word dick but then he saw her attempt at a smile and he smiled too.

"I guess I'm sorry for being a dick?"

"So what happens now?" she asked.

"We kiss and make up?" Jim replied hopefully. He was no longer as sure of her as he had been before, but he knew more than ever that he wanted her. Rosie was still reeling from her recent panic attack. She had assumed that all her nightmares had come true and that Jim was leaving her.

She could not quite understand what had just happened but managed to focus on the word 'kiss'. Gradually as he held her in his arms and covered her mouth with his own, Rosie began to relax. In the previous moments she had lived through her tearful good bye to Jim, her flight back home in humiliation and her long life ahead as a spinster. She was back with Jim, for the moment, but Rosie now knew that she could not continue to live with him if she could not be herself entirely. Things would have to change. For a start it was his turn to cook dinner.

Chapter Thirteen

It was drawing close to the July Fortnight holidays when Sean O'Loan first considered going to New York to visit Jim. Traditionally the building trade in Northern Ireland came to a stand still for two weeks in the middle of July when the *Marching Season* was at its height. The 12 July commemoration of the 1690 Battle of the Boyne was celebrated by half the population of Northern Ireland. The other half tended to either go on holiday or stay and protest against the 'right of Orange men to walk the Queen's highway'. At this time of year Sean usually spent at least a week in Connemara in Co. Galway fishing. This year, however, he decided that he wanted to see Jim and find out for himself how his younger brother was doing.

After booking his ticket and telling his parents that he was going to New York, Sean was suddenly overcome with a feeling of excitement and anticipation. He was excited about seeing New York and seeing Jim but it also dawned on him that he wanted to see Rosie. He had thought about her often in the past 6 months. He wanted to know what she was doing. He wanted to know about her life. He wanted to talk to her and tease her again and watch her get annoyed with him. Most of all he wanted to see her face. He was not sure if his memory of her was correct. He had no photographs of her to look at and in his memory she had morphed to look like a cross between Dana and Dennis the Menace. He still thought she was an eejit but he could not help but admit that he enjoyed her company.

When Rosie and Jim got word that Sean was coming over they were both delighted. Jim was keen to show his brother what he had achieved since being in New York. He wanted to show off, introduce Sean to his friends and show him that he was an independent man in his own right. He wanted Sean to approve of his life and to finally treat him as an equal instead of a younger brother who he had to 'look out for'. Rosie too was determined to make a favourable impression when Sean arrived. She wanted to wipe the 'sarky smile' of Sean's face when he saw how mature and sophisticated she had become. She also wanted Sean to return home to Mrs O'Loan with glowing reports about how wonderful she was and how happy she had made Jim. She fussed over the apartment buying new bed clothes for the spare room, and pictures and modern ornaments to decorate the rather stark surroundings that she and Jim both loved.

Rosie had not thought about Sean much in the past six months. She was too enthralled with her new life and too in love with Jim to give anything else much consideration. When she did think of Sean it was always with a mild sense of irritation and the desire to 'show him'. Now the closer it came to the day of his arrival the more unsettled Rosie became. She could not understand why she felt so compelled to impress Sean. He made it abundantly clear every time they met that he thought she was an idiot and he never tired in his attempts to ridicule her. Rosie decided that she would dispense with any conversation with Sean that did not involve the weather, work or the well being of their respective relatives. She would not allow him to draw her into any topic of conversation that would annoy her in any way. She did not want to fight with Sean and make Jim feel uncomfortable or torn in his loyalties. She most definitely did not want to give Sean the opportunity to make her look small or petty in front of Jim.

Rosie and Jim both managed to get some time off work on the day Sean was due to arrive in New York. It was a Friday and they were both on holiday for a week. They collected Sean at the airport in a car lent to Jim by a friend. When Sean walked through the departure gate he was looking slightly rough and had clearly had a few drinks on the plane. He saw Rosie first before she saw him. His heart leapt for no reason that he could explain and he immediately attempted to gather himself. Jim ran forward and the two brothers shook hands and then hugged awkwardly before starting to laugh and slap each other on the back while talking at the same time as each other. Rosie walked forward but waited to greet Sean until after his initial contact with his brother. She then smiled at Sean and bid him,

"Welcome to New York."

"Spoken like a native, Rosie' he responded, before approaching her and kissing her gently on the cheek. Rosie's face reddened but she did not know why. The momentary closeness of Sean's body, the faint smell of his aftershave and the stronger smell of alcohol and stale smoke were not particularly pleasant, but still Rosie felt her heart stir when he was near her. His touch was strangely unnerving and comforting at the same time. She had to admit to herself that she was glad to see him.

The journey back to Queens took nearly two hours because the traffic was slow. Sean did not mind. He was too busy looking around and taking in the sights to be impatient. He was also in awe of his brother and how he managed to drive so confidently through the mad New York traffic without killing himself or someone else. Several times Sean screamed at Jim to be careful, before remembering that 'Yanks drive on the wrong side of the road'. Rosie giggled in the back of the car at Sean's reaction. He was clearly not a good passenger and would continually slam his feet on imaginary breaks whenever he felt he was not in control. Jim was also enjoying his new found sense of superiority over his brother. He was the man in charge now.

When they arrived at the apartment in Queens, Sean jumped out of the car relieved to finally be on solid ground. He whispered a prayer of thanks to the Almighty for allowing him to arrive safe and well. Feeling instantly relaxed he quickly found his usual sense of humour and commented to Jim that his driving had improved so much that he should soon be able to take the stabilisers of the car. Rosie laughed while Jim struggled to find a witty retort for his brother. He failed. Instead he muttered,
"Fuck you AND the horse you rode in on!" Rosie and Sean laughed in unison for several seconds before Jim joined in. The holiday had begun.

The next week was spent in a series of escapades involving site seeing, eating, drinking and generally taking the piss out of each other. A new triumvirate was formed. Rosie was again in her element. She excelled in situations where she was the central figure. Sean was out of his comfort zone in New York but, being a seasoned traveller, he never allowed himself to venture into a situation where he was not fully aware of the potential risks. Like Rosie, he had a thirst for new experiences and he enjoyed adventures. Jim found himself to be the sole voice of restraint whenever a new outing was being proposed. On the morning after Sean arrived, Rosie pulled out her *Rough Guide to New York* and proposed that they attempt to visit all of the most famous drinking holes in Manhattan which were listed in the book. The oldest pub, the smallest pub, the one that only sold beer, the hard to find speakeasy in the Village were all mentioned. Jim stated that this was a silly idea and pointed out that their local in Queens was the best pub in New York and suggested they go there. Rosie was horrified.

"We can't bring Sean there" she protested, "he didn't come the whole way to New York to sit in an Irish pub. He wants to see Manhattan, don't you Sean," she said, looking to Sean with appealing eyes that anticipated refusal. Sean was on holiday. He wanted to see as much of New York as possible but, equally, he wanted to enjoy Rosie and Jim's company. He thought Rosie's pub crawl idea was a good one but he did not want to offend Jim. They agreed to spend the day in Manhattan and the evening in the pub in Queens.

For Rosie it was a chance to relive her first weeks in New York, only this time she had an audience to share her thoughts, impressions and feelings with. Sean was inspired by her enthusiasm and impressed by her vast knowledge of the history of most of the main sights they visited. They walked for miles in their search of landmarks listed in Rosie's guide book, stopping now and then to have a coffee or a beer in the pubs pre-chosen by Rosie as their ultimate destination. In the Village they managed to find Chumley's which had been a speakeasy during the time of Prohibition. Sean laughed when he saw the grill still on the door. It felt like he was stepping back into a different era. Jim took a photograph of Sean and Rosie posing outside the door. While Jim shouted 'say shit' Sean casually placed his arm around Rosie and they both smiled for the camera. Rosie was keenly aware of the feeling of Sean's arm around her waist. He appeared to be unmoved by the moment. Rosie felt momentarily confused then laughed inwardly at her own foolishness.

After having a drink in the bar the three young people decided to make their way to back to Fifth Avenue. Jim was glad to leave the old pub; he could not quite see what the appeal was to Rosie. She had been twittering on to Sean about some guy named Steinbeck while they drank their beer. Jim spent the time looking around him and had noticed that the old building was in serious need of reinforcement. As they walked through the Village, Rosie and Sean both drank in the atmosphere and the many sights and sounds of that extraordinary area of Manhattan. Rosie stopped occasionally to look in shop windows and finally Jim couldn't help but complain,

"I knew we would end up shopping!" he sighed. He was now feeling quite hungry. He wanted to eat.

"I've no intentions of going shopping" quipped Rosie in disgust. "There is a nice little bistro near here that does the best calamari in town and we can go to the Empire State building after." Jim and Sean were both relieved that they were not going to be dragged round the shops. After all, they were on holiday and shopping was something that women and eejits did. Sean asked Rosie what calamari was. When she told him his gag reflex was automatic.

"You can't eat squid!" he exclaimed, "that's revolting!" Rosie giggled,

"It's yummy! You can have a sandwich or a spud or something you big cultchie!" Jim agreed with Sean but did not want to appear uncultured, so he advised Sean that they also did a nice lasagne. Sean was relieved. They walked to the bistro and were soon tucking into a very large lunch. Sean laughed when he noticed Rosie's habit of humming while she ate. This had annoyed Jim when he first noticed it but he had long since grown accustomed to it and he now found it quite endearing. He had never mentioned it to Rosie as he did not want to embarrass her. Sean was less sensitive.

"What ya singing Rosie?" he asked, smiling wryly at her.

"I wasn't singing" she replied, genuinely unaware that she had been humming *Endless Love* and looking lovingly at her plate of calamari.

"It sounds to me like you really, really LOVE calamari, Rosie," laughed Sean, "or do you always serenade your food?" Rosie looked blankly at Sean before Jim interrupted and said,

"You were doing your humming thing love."

"Really?" exclaimed Rosie, growing red with embarrassment.'

"Yeah, laughed Sean, "don't give up your day job Rosie, you were out of tune!" Rosie grew even redder with embarrassment. Rosie's biggest regret in life was that she was a truly awful singer. She had the soul of a soprano but the voice of a deranged cow. She was the only person in the history of St Catherine's high school who had been asked to leave the school choir as she was incapable of holding a tune. Rosie loved music but she was practically tone deaf. This did not stop her from singing aloud whenever she could. Usually she sang when there was no one else about, but on more than one occasion, when she'd had too much to drink, Rosie had attempted to entertain the company by singing her favourite song *Moon River*. Her attempts were usually met with squeals of laughter from her friends and cries of 'shut the fuck up' from strangers. Rosie could not contain her embarrassment. She was giving serious consideration to leaving her lunch and running into the toilet when Sean stopped her by asking,

"Do you do requests Rosie?" His mock sincerity was too much for her to cope with. Rosie exploded with laughter and promptly called Sean a 'total git!' For his part Sean could not help but feel that there really was something sweet about Rosie's appalling lack of self-awareness; she was extremely unsophisticated, she used foul language continually, she was badly dressed and often quite scruffy looking, but she was funny and witty and she was very much alive. He realised that she made him feel alive, more alive than he had felt in a very long time.

After lunch they all walked down Bleecker Street and turned left onto Broadway. The afternoon was drawing to a close, when they finally arrived outside the Empire State

Building. Jim had not been there since his first visit last year. His face coloured when he remembered the spectacle he had made of himself then. He recalled the intensity of his feelings at the time, and the longing he had felt for Rosie. Now when he looked at her standing with Sean, teasing him relentlessly, his passion for her peaked again. He could no longer remember the time when he did not find her beautiful. It was as if love had coloured his view of her and made her into a different person. Having once thought her insignificant, he now considered her to be the most perfect woman in the world. At that moment, Rosie looked up and caught him staring lovingly at her. Her heart melted and she smiled back shyly at him. She knew they would make love that night and could not help picturing them together alone. The thought embarrassed her because she was suddenly aware of Sean looking at her too. He had noticed the momentary glance that Rosie and Jim shared. He was compelled to stare though he felt as if he was spying on something very private. A sudden realisation dawned on him. Rosie and Jim were genuinely in love. They had the kind of love that writers and poets wrote about. The sort of love that songs celebrated and operas were composed about. For the first time in his life Sean knew what it was to feel absolute, insane jealousy. His mood changed and he became quiet and withdrawn. Jim did not notice, but Rosie was disturbed by the sudden change in him. She wondered if she had offended him and, when Jim stopped to buy cigarettes at a kiosk, Rosie took the opportunity to ask Sean if he was OK? The look of concern on her face brought Sean to his senses. He smiled at her and said,

"Never better Rosie, sure amin't I here with you and my baby brother in New York enjoying my holiday, WHAT could be wrong?" Inadvertently Sean emphasised the word 'what' and held Rosie's gaze for a moment too long. It was as if he wanted her to question what was wrong with the current scenario. The problem was: there were three people in the picture, and Sean could not help wishing it was Jim that was not there. He wanted to be alone with Rosie and he wanted her to feel the same way. Rosie was confused. She was not stupid. She knew that there was something wrong and she instantly worried that it was her fault. *Had she been flirting with Sean? Could he see the effect that he had on her? Did he know that he made her feel insignificant and irritated and frustrated and confused and excited all at the same time? Did Sean know that she had spent time that morning lying in bed trying to think of interesting things to say to him; hoping that he would be impressed by her wit and intelligence?* Rosie was filled with a sense of foreboding. She knew something was happening and she wanted it to stop. She turned and ran back to the kiosk to find Jim. He was talking to the kiosk owner and when he turned round and Rosie saw his face she felt safe again. He kissed her on the head, and they both walked hand in hand back to where Sean was waiting for them. Sean registered that moment. Nothing had been said, but he knew that Rosie was telling him to back off. He knew that he had frightened her.

Chapter Fourteen

On the second week of his holiday Sean decided he would visit some of the museums in Manhattan. Rosie recommended that he see the Guggenheim because of its fabulous architecture, as much as the treasures it held. They had visited the Metropolitan together, earlier in the week. Jim feigned tiredness to get out of going. Sean had enjoyed chatting to Rosie about history and art. She was by no means an expert but she was very enthusiastic and she listened intently when Sean mentioned things that interested her. Sean had always been a lover of history and had read extensively on many subjects. However, his main interests were architecture and the natural world. He decided to go to the Natural History museum first, and visit the Guggenheim when Rosie and Jim were able to accompany him. He knew that he could not risk spending too much time alone with Rosie. Since the moment outside the Empire State Building, Sean had been careful not to show any further outward sign of the growing attraction he felt for Rosie. She had been awkward around him for a short while, before convincing herself that she had imagined something had passed between them when it hadn't. Sean knew he could not afford to embarrass her again.

Wandering round Manhattan on his own was something that Sean had looked forward to doing when he was planning his holiday. In reality, when Rosie and Jim returned to work and left him to his own devices, he felt bereft somehow. He realised that he missed Rosie when she was not about. He had grown used to the inane drivel she spoke; her continual need to talk about whatever came into her head at any given moment and her unusual take on life. She had asked him once if her chatter annoyed him,

"Not at all, Rosie" he had replied sweetly, "you talk away pet, sure I'm not listening." Rosie had snorted indignantly and pointed out that Sean did not deserve to hear her 'pearls of wisdom'. Sean had looked at her and simply stated,

"Rosie Maguire, you're away with the fairies!" Rosie had laughed. She couldn't argue with that.

The trip to the Guggenheim was planned for Wednesday afternoon, two days before Sean was due to fly home. Rosie and Jim both managed to get the afternoon off, and Rosie was really looking forward to spending time with her two favourite people. She had grown close to Sean during his visit and she wanted to see the Guggenheim again. She was also hoping to bring Sean to see the United Nations Building on 1st Avenue. Rosie loved to sit in the café there and people watch. When she mentioned this to Sean and Jim, Sean was interested. Jim suggested that they go to the pub instead as he did not want to 'waste' his afternoon off. Rosie was irritated with him. She told him he could stay at home if he didn't want to come. Jim was giving serious consideration to the idea when he suddenly became jealous at the thought of Sean and Rosie spending more time alone together. It was not that he did not trust his brother but he was never quite sure about Rosie. He agreed to go to the 'stupid' United Nations Building as long as he was allowed to go to the pub in the evening. Rosie laughed at his lack of dignity in defeat and told him he could go to the pub if he behaved himself when they were out. Jim muttered under his breath that Rosie was 'not the boss of me' before noticing the laughter in her eyes. He smiled then and gave her an energetic push. Rosie stumbled and was saved from falling only by the fact that Sean grabbed her. They all laughed when Rosie feigned distress and advised Jim that she now had a witness to the level of domestic abuse she had to put up with. Sean was particularly amused at the idea of anyone attempting to abuse Rosie. *God love anyone who'd be fool enough to try* he thought to himself.

Sean truly enjoyed the experience of walking round the museum with Rosie by his side making continual little comments on everything she saw. Jim had given up very quickly and had taken himself off to have a cigarette and a coffee, leaving Rosie and Sean alone again for the first time in several days. Sean felt ashamed when he realised that he was glad Jim had left. Rosie felt confused when she realised that she too was relieved when Jim left. He was not good company when he was bored and he had made it quite clear that he was not interested in art or architecture or 'stupid Picasso drawings that look like a youngster done them'. Rosie always felt overwhelmed when in the presence of greatness. She loved to imagine how many famous people had stood where she was standing or how many significant events had taken place in whichever historic place she was visiting: but she was not thinking of historic events or people when Jim left. She was thinking about Sean, leaving to go back to Ireland, and wondering when she would see him again. At that moment Sean turned too look at her. Taking her firmly by the hand he asked her to sit down on a nearby bench. He had something he wanted to give her. Sean took from his pocket a small gift box. Rosie's eyes opened wide; she loved presents. Inside the box was a tiny glass fairy, painted in brilliant colours with tiny wings and a mischievous expression on its face.

"She's lovely" Rosie said, trembling as she examined the fairy, afraid she would break it.

"I just wanted to say thanks for the holiday" muttered Sean, who was not comfortable with gift giving ceremonies. "I saw this in a shop the other day and it reminded me of you."

"Why?" asked Rosie, "because I'm so sweet and delicate and fairy like?"

"No", said Sean quietly, "because you're away with the fairies and I thought it would remind you of where you come from." Rosie did not know what to say. She loved her little fairy already but she was unnerved by Sean's candour, "I am not away with the fairies!" she exclaimed, trying to sound bright and breezy when, in fact, she was struggling to quell a rising tide of hysteria within her.

"I'll miss you Rosie Maguire" Sean said simply.

"I'll miss you too" Rosie replied. Sean bent over and kissed her on the cheek. His touch was electric on her skin and her face burned. Sean smiled at her reaction. He wanted to hold her and kiss her properly, deeply and passionately. Rosie was unable to move. She was fighting back tears of confusion and guilt and a deep desire to be completely alone on a deserted island with Sean. At that moment, Jim came sauntering up and enquired if it was time to go yet. Rosie and Sean both stood up and Rosie said quickly,

"Yes, I think we've seen everything."
Sean could not look at his brother. He needed time to gather himself. He suggested that they all go and have a drink before going to the United Nations Building. Sean needed some liquid refreshment to re-establish his equilibrium. Rosie needed a smoke.

They walked for a while after leaving the museum before finding a bar with a neon shamrock outside, which Jim immediately elected as the chosen spot for their sojourn. Several drinks later, they all stumbled out onto the street laughing. It was now 7 o'clock in the evening and it was too late to go to the United Nations. Jim suggested they get something to eat as he was so hungry he could 'eat the leg aw the lamb aw God!' The mention of food snapped Rosie into action. She was ravenous.
"Oh, yes!" she agreed, I'm feeling a tad peckish too! Sean smiled at her understatement. He knew Rosie loved her grub and he did not relish the idea of having to cope with her when she was hungry. They walked for a while before finding a tiny little Italian restaurant. Rosie was initially loath to enter the place, as she was sure it would be expensive. Sean insisted that he wanted to treat her and Jim to their dinner before he left and, after an appropriate level of protest on the part of Jim and Rosie, it was agreed that they would have dinner in the restaurant and blow the rest of Sean's American dollars on a cab home to Queens.

The meal was lovely; Rosie entertained Sean and Jim with stories of her high school exploits and chatted about her family and home. The alcohol made Rosie feel nostalgic and she waxed melancholy towards the end of the evening. Sean noticed her sudden change in mood but waited until Jim excused himself to 'use the powder room' before asking, "What's wrong?" Rosie remained quiet for a moment before saying,

"I miss home sometimes."

"It would be strange if you didn't Rosie" Sean stated, matter-of-factly.

"I'm very happy here" she added quickly, "but I miss the banter and the craic with the girls . . . . and I miss my mummy and daddy." Sean looked intently at her troubled face. When she was quiet and thoughtful, as she was now, Sean noticed that she was prettier than was her usual state. At that moment, he thought she was quite lovely, yet he longed to be the one to restore her to her usual self. He could not bear to see the pain in her eyes. He felt that he was somehow responsible, for at least part of it. His presence in her happy world had caused her to doubt herself and he knew that he had damaged, perhaps for ever, Rosie's belief in her relationship with Jim. He felt like a cad, an old fashioned, stereotypical cad who had set out to seduce his brother's lover.

"Rosie, everyone gets homesick after a while. You should think of coming home for a visit soon so you can see your family and all."

"I would" she said, "but I'm afraid of not getting back into the country. My visa expired months ago." Sean empathised with her dilemma. She really had given up a lot for his brother. Sean wondered if Jim realised just what he had in Rosie.

"Does Jim know how you feel, Rosie?" he asked.

"Oh no!" she exclaimed emphatically, "I couldn't tell him. He might think that I didn't want to be here, and I do but . . . . I guess I would prefer it if I knew we were going home together soon. I love New York, but like, you couldn't live here forever. Yanks are mad!"

"I know" said Sean sympathetically, "and people from Northern Ireland are the sanest people on the planet!"

"We are that" she laughed, "no better people in the world! Pity we can't learn to get along better with each other." Sean nodded, adding,

"That'll be the day!"

When Jim returned, Sean paid the bill and they left the restaurant. Rosie had smiled radiantly when Jim sat down. Sean noticed how quickly she was able to hide her distress. She was protecting Jim. For some reason Sean was angry. He felt it was Rosie who needed protecting. It was an inherent belief that he held. No man should be the cause of a woman's tears and, if he was, he should bloody well make sure he fixed it right and quick. Jim was completely unaware of the myriad feelings that Rosie was capable of. This was not entirely his fault. Rosie chose to hide many of her thoughts and dreams from him. Sean wanted to shake him. He wanted Jim to realise that part of Rosie was slowly decaying in New York. Yes, she loved to meet new people and experience new things but she also needed to be with her own kind who accepted her and loved her no matter what mood she was in. Sean realised that Rosie had somehow managed to create a sort of half life for herself in New York. She was Rosie the witty, pretty, quirky love interest of Jim O'Loan. The other Rosie was hidden from view and was only visible in moments of weakness or to those who chose to look. It seemed to Sean that Rosie was wasted on his brother. Jim could never really appreciate her because he did not know all of her. Rosie would never let him truly see her; she was afraid that he would not like or understand what he saw. She tended to avoid arguments with him as she did not like to hurt his feelings. She never truly relaxed when he was around. She was always on her guard in case she would say or do something that irritated or revolted him. Sometimes she talked in her sleep and this was a constant source of worry to her. She was afraid that she would say something wild or weird. She needn't have worried. When she talked in her sleep, if Jim noticed at all, he simply told her to 'shush love' and patted her head.

They walked for a while after leaving the restaurant. It was extremely hot outside and Sean longed to feel a cool breeze or a drop of rain or even a cold wind, anything that would relieve the oppressive stagnant heat that enveloped him. Sean noticed that Rosie maintained her 'Jim' persona. She was teasing him and making him laugh and was smiling sweetly whenever he condescended to throw her a glance. Sean wanted to hit her now. He controlled his irritation. What was the point of getting angry? He was going home and whatever happened between Rosie and Jim would no longer be his concern. Suddenly Rosie squealed with delight pointing to the other side of the road.

"Oh look! It's an ice cream stand! Can we get one?" she yelped, hopping about like a small child and pulling at Jim's sleeve. Jim looked at Sean and they both raised their eyes to heaven.

"OK!" sighed Jim, nodding at Sean. Before either of them could stop her Rosie ran out onto the road, her eyes focused entirely on the ice cream cart. Sean was first to react lunging forward and grabbing furiously at Rosie's arm. Jim followed suit. As Sean managed to drag Rosie back to the sidewalk, Jim turned into the flow of on-coming traffic. There was a sudden screech of breaks: the belated blare of a car horn, and finally an horrendous thud and Jim was gone. Weeks later, Rosie would recall the look of horror on the cab driver's face as Jim's body descended onto the bonnet of his cab. It would haunt her dreams for eternity. At that moment, however, all she could see was lifeless form of Jim, his open, upside down eyes staring at her blankly. Rosie remained frozen to the spot. Sean ran to the cab. Trembling he fumbled at Jim's neckline trying to find a pulse as he had seen done on numerous occasions on TV. The cab driver joined him and soon there was a gathering of passers-by assembled at the scene. Someone called 911 and, from the crowd, an officious looking man appeared carrying the obligatory case which indicated that he was a doctor. He examined Jim briefly before turning to Sean. Rosie saw him shake his head and pat Sean gently on the shoulder. At that moment her knees buckled, and she crumpled forward onto the ground. Sean walked slowly towards her and knelt down beside her. He folded her body into his arms and rocked her gently. He held her until the ambulance and NYPD arrived. She did not cry.

Chapter Fifteen

Two weeks later, Jim's funeral was held at the Chapel in Tullycross. Sean had organised everything from the American end, while his family had taken care of arrangements back home. Ricardo and Cecelia were invaluable during that time: Ricardo assisting Sean with arrangements while Cecelia cared for Rosie as if she was her own daughter. An Irish/American charitable organisation in New York organised for Jim's body to be flown home and helped pay the costs. Neither Jim nor Rosie had any sort of health or life insurance and the whole process had been expensive and difficult. For the most part, Sean maintained a stoic, steel like strength, dealing with everyone and everything calmly and sensitively. His Achilles' heel was Rosie. There were moments when he had been concerned for her sanity, such was the intensity of Rosie's reaction to Jim's death.

When they returned to the apartment from the morgue the evening after the accident, alone for the first time since Jim's death, Rosie could not bear to look at Sean. He thought that she was angry with him but, the truth was, she could think only that she had been responsible for his brother's death. Her grief was tempered by an all consuming guilt. She couldn't look anybody in the eye; least of all the brother of the man she had killed. Sean attempted to talk to her while making tea and insisting she 'eat something'. Rosie thanked him but stated that she needed to be alone for a while.

"You need to get some sleep Sean" she said quietly, "I'll be OK." Sean was afraid to leave her alone. When she went to bed, he searched the flat for tablets or medication that she could overdose on and removed all the sharp knives he could find. He knew that Rosie was beyond despair. She had hardly spoken a word since the previous evening. The doctor in the hospital had treated her for shock and sedated her. Cecelia had insisted that both she and Sean spend what was left of the night with her and Ricardo. Rosie had slept a drug induced sleep and had felt nothing. Sean had not shut his eyes since Tuesday. It was now late Thursday evening.

During that first night alone Rosie had wakened screaming. Sean ran to her room and held her while she cried for hours. She eventually fell asleep again. Sean remained with her, lying by her side, occasionally stroking her hair. He finally fell asleep too but woke suddenly in the morning before Rosie. He could not help but gaze at her face as she slept. She was quiet now and her sleep appeared to be undisturbed. Sean hoped she would not waken. He could not bear to see her eyes. He crept quietly from the room and decided to take a shower. When he had shaved and dressed he walked into the living room only to behold Rosie standing on the window ledge overlooking the street. Her nightdress fluttered in the morning breeze. She did not hear him come into the room. Her eyes were transfixed on the ground three storeys below. Sean's heart stopped momentarily. His initial response was to run to her but something stopped him. She was too near the edge. He walked quietly towards her but she turned before he could reach her. His eyes pleaded with her and something in his aspect stopped her.

"Don't Rosie" he said gently, "I need you to come back." Rosie began to shake. Before she could move Sean grabbed her wrist firmly and pulled her forward into his arms. It was too much for Sean. The internal dam which had been retaining his emotions suddenly broke. Holding her by the shoulders, he thrust her from him and shook her like a rag doll. The look of terror on her face stopped him, and he let go of her as if she was on fire. He turned his back and it was then that Rosie saw him begin to shake violently. At that moment she felt an overwhelming urge to comfort him. Standing behind him, she placed her arms around his body and drew him to her. At first Sean tried to shrug her off but she held on placing her cheek against his back. He was shaking uncontrollably. They stood in that mode until Sean ceased to tremble and finally turned to face her.

"I'm sorry" she said quietly, "it won't happen again." He was not convinced but he knew that at least she had returned. She was not intact. She would never again be the Rosie of before but at least she had come back to earth, back to reality, back to him.

Sitting in the chapel at Tullycross surrounded by friends and relatives, Rosie thought about all that had happened. She missed Jim every second of the day but still the overriding emotion she felt was guilt. Mrs Maguire had hugged her closely when she and Sean arrived home. The welcome was, of course, subdued, but there was no sign of anger or accusation in the older woman's manner. It didn't matter. Rosie had enough anger and accusations to level at herself, enough to last a life time. She was consumed with guilt. The words 'if only' repeated themselves continually in her mind. *If only she had not insisted that Jim go to the museum that day; if only she hadn't run onto the street; if only she had not gone to New York in the first place; if only she had begged Jim to stay in Ireland instead of telling him to go to New York; if only it had been her and not him that had been killed; if only she had never been born in the first place.* It was during moments like this that Rosie imagined that everyone and everything in the world would be better off if only she had never existed. She saw herself as a weak, selfish, loathsome, snivelling creature with no purpose in life other than to plague those around her. She repeatedly imagined what it would be like to have done with it all. She imagined jumping in front of a moving train like Anna Karenina, or falling from the top of cliff into an ocean where she would be swept away from all those who knew her and knew what she had done.

While sitting in the chapel, Rosie realised that she had not been alone at all since that first night she had spent with Sean in the apartment after Jim's death. Sean had insisted that someone be with her at all times. In New York he relied on Cecelia, and her connections, to sit with Rosie. Back home, he had stated clearly to Mr and Mrs Maguire that Rosie should not be left unsupervised, even for a moment. They knew what he meant without having to go into details. The Rosie that returned to them from New York was a stranger. Mrs Maguire had always been able to read her daughter like an open book, but that Rosie had gone. In her place was a living, breathing ghost. She was able to carry on with only the most basic tasks of daily living. She breathed in and out, she walked, she was able to make monosyllabic responses to questions, she could wash and dress herself and she could eat. Beyond that, Rosie was incapable of connecting with anyone or feeling anything other than the pain of regret, shame and guilt. The entire Maguire family grieved for the Rosie they had lost. Ellie, who had practically moved into the Maguire home, had barely left Rosie's side since her return. For the most part, it did not matter to Rosie who was with her. She was aware of all that went on around her but only just. She was trapped in a prison inside herself and as time went by the walls grew larger and stronger. The one person whose absence she noted was Sean. He had become her lifeline in the past two weeks. She drew strength form his presence. She watched him from her *cell* following his every move whenever he was near. She held onto him now as they sat together in the chapel. She needed his physical presence to keep her grounded. One look from him was enough to keep her rooted to the seat. If he had not been there she would have run away screaming from the unbearable scene that played out in front of her. She was at Jim's funeral. His parents and brothers, their wives and children sat together as a unit comforting each other. His friends, male and female, wept openly. Rosie's own family were also able to express the grief they felt for the loss of Jim. Strangers who did not know him were saddened by the story in the local paper about the young man who had been cut down in the prime of life. Only Rosie could not show her feelings. If she had, she would have been locked up.

The mass came to an end and the priest walked down the aisle followed by Jim's brothers and father who flanked his coffin. Sean walked behind with his mother on one side and Rosie on the other. Both women needed him to hold them up. Mrs O'Loan's grief was evident as she wept openly. Rosie hung her head. Many in the congregation wanted to reach out to her to pay their respects, but Rosie could not see or hear anyone. She was in a trance. She remained dry eyed until the moment when Jim's body was being lowered into his grave. It was then that Rosie felt it. It was as if the last fragments of her heart were being annihilated. Inside she was screaming Jim's name. Ellie was first to notice her face and she reacted quickly. She knew that it would be wrong for Rosie to make a scene at the graveside. Ellie quickly pulled Anne by the hand and whispered to her,

"We need to get Rosie away." Anne too reacted quickly. They moved towards Rosie and were able to shuffle her away before Rosie's legs buckled under her. They took her to the nearest waiting limo which had been hired to bring the nearest relatives to the funeral. Inside the car, Rosie screamed Jim's name repeatedly, reliving the first moments when he had been killed and saying the words she had not been able to say before. Ellie and Anne hugged her and held her in turn until the sobbing subsided and Rosie stopped trembling. By this stage others were starting to make their way to the car park as the funeral was over. Sean opened the door of the limo and looked at Rosie. Without saying anything he got into the car. Ellie moved over and he sat beside Rosie.

"It wasn't your fault Rosie" he whispered quietly into her ear, putting his arm around her. "It was Sean" she said. "I loved him . . . . and . . . I killed him."

"It was an accident" stated Sean emphatically. Rosie knew he was trying to convince himself as much as he was trying to convince her. Sean was only just beginning to assemble the threads of his feelings about Jim's death, but already they were growing into a mesh of guilt and self loathing that he wore like a horse hair shirt.

Chapter Sixteen

It was the last day of August and Ellie was preparing to visit
Rosie. She had not seen her the day before. It was the first
day since Rosie's return to Ireland that Ellie had stayed away.
She needed to be alone. She was exhausted and wanted
to spend time with her own family. Ellie also needed to
make plans. She had been accepted into Queen's University
and needed to sort out accommodation. She was worried
about telling Rosie she would be moving to Belfast. Ellie's
mother drove her out to the Maguire house. Mrs McKeown
was concerned for her own daughter. She was proud that
Ellie was going to university and wanted to make a fuss
of her, but it was impossible under the circumstances. Mrs
McKeown, like everyone else, felt the tragedy of Jim's death,
but her main concern was her own daughter's wellbeing.
She did not like to see Ellie looking so tired and drawn.

Rosie was sitting in the garden at the back of the house
when Ellie arrived. She smiled weakly at her friend. She was
genuinely glad to see her. Ellie sat down beside Rosie on the
garden seat,
"How are you?' she asked tentatively. Rosie looked at her
and sighed deeply.

"I don't really know" she shrugged. "I keep thinking that I should feel different . . . . you know . . . . I should be crying or something but I don't feel anything right now."

"Do you want a smoke?" Ellie asked, hoping that Rosie would offer her a cup of tea. She did. When Rosie returned with the tea, she and Ellie lit up a cigarette and puffed silently for several minutes without talking. Finally Ellie said,

"I got into Queens." She waited for a response from Rosie. Rosie was stricken by the news, but she recovered quickly and smiled at Ellie,

"That's great Ellie, I'm so pleased for you" she said. Rosie's initial hesitation had not gone unnoticed. Ellie thought of all the times they had planned to go to university together.

"You know you could still go Rosie, if you sit your 'A' levels next year. We could get a flat together then." Rosie smiled. She had not thought of going to university for a long time. Suddenly she realised that she was unemployed, unqualified and pretty much unprepared for any sort of work. Ellie continued,

"You could go to Armagh tech this year. Lots of people we know are repeating their 'A' levels, and you could reapply to Queen's for next year." Rosie thought about it. She really could not bear to do anything at the moment, but common sense made her see that she could not just stay at home living off her parents and doing nothing. Neither could she think about looking for full-time work at the moment. The thought of holding down a job was too frightening to consider. At least if she was going to tech she would be out of the house most days and she could justify her existence. Rosie turned to Ellie slowly and said,

"Yes, I think I will." Ellie was relieved.

When Ellie told Mr and Mrs Maguire that Rosie was going to repeat her 'A' levels they were delighted. Mrs Maguire knew her daughter could not stay idle for long, and that she needed a distraction from the heartbreak she was going through. Mr Maguire was just glad that Rosie was doing something other than staring into space. It made him feel very uncomfortable and inadequate. He wanted to help Rosie; Mr Maguire was a very handy man, but the one thing he couldn't do was fix a broken heart.

The following day Rosie signed up to do her 'A' Levels in the technical college in Armagh. She chose to do English Literature, Maths and Psychology. It would be a very tough year ahead, and Rosie knew that she had a lot of catching up to do if she wanted to get the grades needed to get into Queen's. Rosie wanted to speak to Sean and tell him about her plans, but he had not called in a couple of days. He was back at work now and was very busy. Rosie could not help feeling that he was also trying to distance himself from her. She realised now how difficult the last few weeks must have been for him. She had taken nothing to do with the preparations for Jim's funeral. She had not even packed her own clothes for returning to Ireland. She had been propelled gently along by a troop of people with Sean as their captain, guiding her and protecting her at all times. How he must have suffered she thought? His own grief had been pushed aside by the overwhelming need to get Jim home and to keep Rosie on track. A deep sense of awe and gratitude began to grow inside Rosie when she thought of Sean. He had become a hero in her eyes. He had saved her life and now she wanted to thank him over and over again for all he had done.

For his part, Sean was not feeling particularly heroic. He was struggling with the ambivalent feelings he had for Rosie Maguire. Every time he thought of her he became confused. He was aware of Rosie's growing dependence on him, but he knew that her feelings were grounded in gratitude and had nothing to do with romantic attachment. This caused him relief and regret in equal measure. He did not want to love Rosie. She was his dead brother's girlfriend. She thought of him as a 'friend'. She could not love him back. Apart from that, Sean could never quite get over the notion that Rosie was a bit unhinged and always had been. He believed that Rosie Maguire would never be anything other than trouble to any man who loved her. He did not blame Rosie for Jim's death, though part of him wanted to. The fact was Sean blamed himself. It had been his idea that Jim should go to New York, and it was him who had manipulated Jim into leaving when he wanted to stay at home with Rosie. More than anything however, what haunted Sean was that moment on the sidewalk in Manhattan when he had run after Rosie into the oncoming traffic. Sean had run after Rosie, but, he was convinced that Jim had not. Jim had run after Sean. Ever since he had been little, Jim had idolised his older brother and when Sean ran to grab Rosie, Jim had not been looking at Rosie, he had just followed Sean instinctively. Sean had not shared this with anyone. There was no one he could share it with. Rosie, over the past weeks, had intermittently shared all of her inner most feelings of pain and regret with just about anyone who would listen. She had been petted and stroked and reassured that it was not her fault, but Sean had held his guilt quietly inside himself. It bore down on him like bricks in a hob which got heavier the longer he carried it.

Rosie was a continual source of pain to him. He could not love her openly and he was growing increasingly frustrated by her new found adoration of him. The thought of her tormented his waking hours and she haunted his dreams at night. Rosie was oblivious to his feelings. Rosie was pretty much oblivious to the feelings of anyone other than herself at that time. Sean knew that he could not expect anything else from Rosie. After all, her heart was 'in the grave' as she kept telling him. His pride hurt. He knew that he could no longer play *friends* with Rosie. He knew he must get away from her or she would be the undoing of him. He decided to speak to her about it.

Sean telephoned Rosie that night and asked if she wanted to go for a drive with him 'to get out of the house.' Rosie was immediately worried. Sean sounded stressed. She automatically said 'yes' and Sean agreed to call for her in half an hour. Rosie stopped to look at herself in the bathroom mirror as she was getting washed and dressed. She did not look good. Her eyes had deep, dark circles around them and she had lost almost a stone in weight. Her skin was dry and pale. She wanted to look nice for Sean, but felt guilty because she did. Why should she be so worried about how she looked? The love of her life was dead and she would never again care for another man. She decided that it was nothing but shear vanity to be so concerned about her appearance. Still, she put a layer of make up on and brushed her hair until it shone. When she heard the door bell ring her heart leapt and again she was stung by a sharp stab of shame. She answered the door and invited Sean in. He went immediately to speak to Rosie's parents. They were glad to see him; they were glad to see anyone who would provide a distraction from the abyss of pain that was Rosie. After speaking to Mr and Mrs Maguire, and the rest of the family who were watching television in the living room, Sean stated that he and Rosie would 'not be long.' Rosie grabbed her coat and said 'cheerio' to her family. There was a collective sigh of relief from all the Maguire's as she left. Sadness did not sit well in the household, and the younger Maguire's were becoming increasingly distressed living with Rosie's very audible grieving. Rosie, for the most part, was oblivious to their discomfort, but occasionally she would notice how Ryan and Orlagh left the room when she entered, and Shane would make an excuse to go out if she began talking about Jim. For the first time in their lives, all three of the young Maguire's were looking forward to going back to school after the summer holidays. Anything was better than being with Rosie and her all consuming grief.

Sean held the car door open for Rosie and she thanked him as she got in. He did not ask her where she wanted to go, he just drove. Rosie made small talk as she often did when she was nervous. Sean responded in kind but she knew that he was thinking of something else. He stopped the car beside the river Bann and they both got out to go for a walk. Eventually they sat down near the river bank. It was a lovely evening. The sun was still quite high in the sky and Rosie enjoyed feeling it's warmth on her face. There was a slight breeze which invigorated her; she was glad to be outside. As usual Rosie was first to speak,
"What's up doc?" she asked, trying to sound casual. Her heart ached more than usual at that moment, but she did not know why. Sean stared at her. He wanted to tell her everything. He wanted her to know how he felt and to he

wanted her to understand. More than anything he wanted to take her in his arms and do unspeakable things to her. He searched her face for any sign of desire or passion. She could not hold his gaze and looked away from him. Before he could speak, she again interrupted his train of thought and blurted out,

"I've decided to go to Armagh tech to do my 'A' Levels. I should be starting next week." Sean was taken aback.

"Why?" he asked simply.

"I want to go to Queens next year" she replied.

"To do what?" asked Sean.

"So I can be a student and me and Ellie can get a flat and I can move out of home" she stated.

"Yes" Sean replied, "but what are you going to do, Rosie . . . I mean, when you grow up?" Rosie stared blankly at him.

"Oh you mean what subject am I going to study?"

"Yes" sighed Sean impatiently.

"Oh, probably Women's Studies or English Literature or something like that."

"Rosie, what the hell sort of job is that going to get you?" Sean snapped. He was impatient with her. He had brought her here to have a serious conversation about their respective futures and he felt that she had derailed him. Rosie was hurt by his tone of voice. She stood up and began to walk away from him. Sean sighed deeply and went after her.

"I'm sorry Rosie" he said, touching her arm. Rosie turned to him and managed to produce a weak smile. She could not bear to snap back at him. She just wanted everything to be relaxed between them.

"I guess I haven't given it a lot of thought Sean; I just know that I can't live at home and do nothing and the only work I'm used to is in restaurants, and if I keep working in the food industry I will be the size of a house before I'm twenty-five." Sean could not help but smile again. Rosie did love her grub.

"I guess I just can't help worrying about you" he said.

"That's because you saved my life Sean and you now feel responsible for me." It was the first time she had ever said that to him. Again he felt burdened by her gratitude. She had been more fun when she disliked him. She had bickered with him and stood up to him and taunted him. Now she was looking adoringly at him as if he was Santa Clause or the Pope or a giant ice cream. Sean was becoming increasingly frustrated with her. He had an overwhelming desire to hurt her at that moment. He wanted to snap her out of her delusion and make her see him properly. He knew that his timing was all wrong but he could not help himself. He reached out and grabbed Rosie and kissed her fully on the month. Rosie did not have time to think, her mind went blank completely and her body responded with shear animal instinct. She reacted to his kiss instantly. Blood raced through her veins, her heart thumped and she trembled all over. Encouraged by her response Sean continued. He could not stop. His hands pulled her closer and his kisses covered her face and neck. Rosie ached for him now. She wanted to feel his skin next to her skin. She wanted his hands on her body. Her eyes flashed a look at his which they both understood instinctively. In an instant they were lying on the ground and Sean's hand was winding its way up her thigh beneath the flimsy cotton of her skirt. Rosie could not stop herself, even though she knew she should. Her passion for Sean had come from somewhere unknown to her: from the depths of her soul, or from hell. Every fibre of her being ached for him now and there was not a rational or reasonable thought in her head at that moment. Sean too was devoid of any sense or guilt or shame. His only feeling was pleasure as his hands covered Rosie's body and he gathered her too him. Everything felt right for once. He felt this was where he should be. He spoke gently too her, repeating her name between guttural groans of desire. From somewhere deep inside him, he heard a voice saying,

"I love you Rosie." He did not realise at first that he had spoken aloud until he noticed Rosie had frozen. She sat up suddenly leaving Sean reeling back.

"What's wrong?" he said, glancing round to see if the ground was still beneath them. Rosie looked at him as her eyes filled with tears,

"We can't do this Sean, its wrong."

"It didn't feel wrong to me" he blurted out, still unsure what had happened. "I want you Rosie and you want me, so what's the problem?" he asked, trying to sound less aggressive.

"Jim" she said quietly. Hearing his dead brother's name spoken aloud Sean was immediately restored to his former self. The guilt and shame and grief returned and his passion for Rosie was replaced by self-loathing and embarrassment. He had overstepped the mark. Rosie was not able to recover her equanimity as easily. She was still flushed with desire and continued to tremble for several moments as they sat in silence. Finally she looked at Sean and said,

"There is no point in me saying that I don't want you Sean . . . . I think I made it quite clear that I do . . . . but I cannot love anyone at the moment, and I don't want anyone getting hurt, especially not you." Sean was instantly irritated. He thought of all the girls he had finished with in the past simply because they seemed to be getting too serious. He thought of the various lines he had used when he wanted to disengage himself from a relationship. He was pretty sure he had said something similar to what Rosie had just said to him. *What goes around comes around* he sighed to himself. It was humiliating.

"I don't REALLY love you" he said, trying to sound flippant, "I was just carried away by your beauty and wit and charm!"

"Fuck you Sean O'Loan, ya sarky git" she snapped at him, before smiling and thumping him on the shoulders with her fists. He grabbed her wrists and pulled her towards him. She buried her head in his chest and they both sighed deeply.

"I'd rather fuck you" he said quietly as he bent to down to look at her. Rosie laughed for the first time in weeks,

"You are a fiend" she said, smiling up at him.

"And you Rosie, are a wee girl with a lot of growing up to do . . . but for once I think you are right" he stated matter-of-factly.

"What do you mean?" she said, sounding surprised.

"I think we shouldn't see each other for a while. You're going back to *school* and I am busy at work and perhaps we need to take time to . . . recover from all that's happened. Rosie was confused. She had not anticipated that Sean would ever leave her. She needed him. She depended on him. She wanted him, but she was sure she did not love him. Well, not in the way she had loved Jim. She could never love anyone the way she had loved Jim, could she? And yet just now she had been ready to have sex with the brother of her dead idol, and Jim hardly cold in his grave. What sort of a person did that make her? *A total slut for a start* thought Rosie as she sighed deeply while fresh waves of embarrassment and shame coloured her body from her face to her toes. She wanted to disappear. *Oh when will They finally invent that Beam me up gadget from Star Trek* thought Rosie to herself.

"Take me home Sean" she whispered.

"OK Rosie" replied Sean, unable to think of anything else to say.

When they arrived back at the Maguire house, Sean kept the engine running in the car. He wanted a quick get away. Rosie seemed reluctant, however, to get out of the car. She turned to look at him but he kept his eyes riveted on the steering wheel.

"Can we still be friends Sean?' she asked quietly. *Oh boke* thought Sean. It was such a clichéd line.

"Off course Rosie" he replied sweetly, "perhaps we could do yoga or go shopping together?" he added, unable to keep the bitterness from his tone.

"There's no need to be so sarcastic" retorted Rosie, anger burning in her throat. She was hurt, yet she had to admit it had been a stupid thing to say. A man like Sean did not have female friends. He had girlfriends and he had buddies but they both had entirely different purposes in his life.

"I'm sorry Rosie" he said, less sarcastically, "I guess it's just a bit too hard for me to be around you. I don't know why, but I have an uncontrollable desire to put my hands on you whenever you are near me. Mind you, most times I just want to put my hands round your throat and squeeze tightly." He laughed as he noted Rosie's reaction. She had wanted to hear him talk about how much he desired her. She wanted him to talk about his love for her, even though she was ashamed to hear it. She was furious when he started to joke about a subject that was so dear to her: herself! The fury passed quickly when Rosie noticed the bitter twist to Sean's mouth. He was joking with her, but he was hurt and she could not bear to hurt him any more.

"OK git face, sworn enemies it is then!" she quipped, as she opened the door and started to get out of the car.

"Yeah, Rosie, sworn enemies . . . . forever" sighed Sean, as he bent over and kissed her on the nose. He smiled knowingly at her as he said goodbye. A tiny glimmer of hope formed in Rosie's heart as she thought of the years ahead. After all, she was only eighteen, and no matter what Sean thought about her, Rosie knew she was not the only one who was *away with the fairies.*

Epilogue

Rosie walked slowly down the isle of the chapel. Her father walked proudly by her side. Family and friends turned around in their seats to catch a glimpse of the bride, shimmering in silk. Everyone was smiling. Rosie looked to the front of the chapel. A tall, dark man was waiting for her. She could not see his face. Inside Rosie was hysterical. Fear and panic consumed her. She wanted to turn and run away. All the months of preparation and anticipation suddenly paled into insignificance. *What am I doing?* She screamed inwardly. She wondered if people could read her thoughts. *This is wrong. I've made a mistake. I can't do this. What the fuck is happening?* She wanted to run, but her feet were rooted to the ground. As usual Rosie's response to any crisis situation was to freeze. She was incapable of flight and was too self-conscious to fight. The entrance hymn finished, and the murmuring in the chapel dulled. Instinctively Rosie turned round to look at the back of the chapel. The doors were shut tight. She was trapped. She turned back and looked at the priest at the front of the chapel waiting for her. In Rosie's mind he had morphed into her gaoler. Suddenly the chapel doors opened making a loud creaking sound. Everyone turned to see who the late comer was.

Sean O'Loan entered the chapel and strode purposefully down the isle towards Rosie. He was clearly agitated, almost angry. He looked accusingly at Rosie but did not speak. Rosie turned away and looked towards her intended groom. His back was still turned to her as if he had not heard Sean enter the chapel. Slowly the unknown groom turned to look at Rosie. He had no face. Instead there was a black hole where his features should have been. In an instant the black hole was replaced by the most malevolent pair of eyes Rosie had ever seen. A face gradually formed into a horribly distorted version of Jim O'Loan's features. He was glaring and pointing a bony, accusing finger at Rosie.

Rosie woke screaming. Within a minute Ellie was sitting on the bed, her arm firmly planted round Rosie's shoulder, comforting her and encouraging her to calm down. When Rosie finally settled, Ellie asked what her nightmare was about.

"Oh. Ellie, it was awful" sobbed Rosie, "I dreamt I was getting . . . . married." Ellie smiled wryly,

"How awful for you" she said sympathetically. "Who was the intended victim?"

"It was Jim, but his face was awful. He was really creepy and evil looking and Sean O'Loan was there and he wasn't best pleased."

"I don't know why you don't just shag that man and get it over with, Rosie. You are obviously in love with him and he's crazy about you" said Ellie, smiling wryly.

"No he isn't Ellie. He's a total git who is never done annoying me" replied Rosie.

"That's because he knows you are full of mad dog shit!" stated Ellie, emphatically. "He is the only man I know that isn't taken in by your crap. He knows everything about you Rosie, and he still likes you. Personally, I think he has very poor taste but I suppose no one's perfect!" Rosie thought for a moment before replying,

"Do you really think he loves' me?" she asked, searching Ellie's face for a sincere reaction.

"God love his wit, but I think he does" stated Ellie. "The poor man can't seem to do without you."

"He does all right" muttered Rosie. "Sure I haven't seen him in weeks."

"That's because the last time you did see him you told him you were planning to move to California. What did you expect him to do? He's not going to wait forever for you to wise up and settled down."

It was 1989. Ellie and Rosie were sharing a flat in Malone Avenue in Belfast. Rosie had just finished her three year degree course at Queen's, and Ellie was working in Belfast Central Library in the city centre. She had qualified the previous year and was already earning a lot more money than Rosie. She even had a car which made Rosie extremely jealous. The girls were planning to go home for the weekend. *Bagatelle* were due to play in the hotel in Tullymore that night, and Rosie and Ellie both had tickets to go. Rosie was glad to have finally finished studying. She longed to get a good job and earn some money so she could buy her own car and could travel more. Her part time job in Lavery's bar in Shaftsbury Square did not pay enough to keep Rosie in the style to which she wanted to become accustomed. Rosie was permanently broke; she could barely afford her share of rent on the flat.

The girls had breakfast and, after washing and dressing, they both packed their weekend bags and headed home in Ellie's Fiat Panda. When they arrived at Rosie's house, Mrs Maguire made the girls a cup of tea and a full Irish breakfast. As she cooked, she regaled Rosie and Ellie with stories of the family and the *goings on* in town. Rosie was glad to be home. She missed her mother while she was in Belfast. She especially missed her mother's cooking. Rosie was only half listening to her mother's chatter. She was more interested in the food that was being prepared.

". . . and I believe Sean O'Loan has brought a girl home with him from Spain" said Mrs Maguire, looking at Rosie out of the side of her eye to gage her reaction. Rosie's ears pricked up at the sound of Sean's name. *That got her attention* thought Mrs Maguire, glancing knowingly at Ellie. Ellie smiled at Mrs Maguire. She knew instinctively what she was about. Rosie was silent for a moment.

"Oh" she said finally, "what's she like?"

"Oh she's a real beauty, they met while Sean was on holiday and he has brought her home to meet the family. I saw her at mass the other day."

"He took her to mass!" exclaimed Rosie, "the ol' hypocrite!"

"I think he just wanted to show her off" said Mrs Maguire, "she is really very pretty and she seems to be a lovely person. I hope they will be very happy. He deserves a nice girl. I have always thought he was a good lad . . ."

Rosie's mother continued to talk at length about the merits of Sean O'Loan and the Spanish beauty he had brought home to Ireland. Before the end of their meal Ellie and Mrs O'Loan where discussing the wedding and wondering would it be in Ireland or Spain. They were also wondering if they would be invited. Rosie was fuming. She longed to speak to Sean and find out if it was true but she knew that there was nothing she could say to him that would not sound selfish and childish and jealous. She could not understand her anger, much less her jealousy. Her feelings were extremely mixed up. Several strands of thoughts ran through her head at one time, but all ended with the same paradox. She could not be in love with Sean because she was still in love with Jim: but then how could she still be in love with Jim when he was dead? If Jim were still alive would she still be in love with him? If Sean were not about to get married to another woman would she even be thinking about him? Rosie had to admit to herself that what bothered her most was change. She was happy enough to have Sean in the background of her life, believing that he loved her despite himself. She could not, however, face the fact that she might be in love with him. What really horrified her though, was the thought that Sean might be in love with another woman.

Ellie looked at Rosie's stricken face. She then noticed that Rosie had not finished her breakfast. This was deeply concerning. Mrs Maguire also noticed the food left on Rosie's plate. She wondered should she call a doctor. The last time Rosie had left food on her plate she was eight years old and was suffering from an attack of tonsillitis.
"Are you OK Rosie?" asked Mrs Maguire. The concern in her voice brought Rosie back to reality.
"Never better" she said, smiling at her mother. Mrs Maguire noticed the tears in her eyes but said nothing. She decided to leave the girls to talk alone for a while. Ellie was less diplomatic.

"Are you for real Rosie?" she snapped, as soon as Mrs Maguire left the kitchen. "Are you jealous because Sean had finally met someone?"

"I am not jealous!" said Rosie emphatically, but she knew she was lying and so did Ellie.

"Well that's just typical, Rosie! Now that Sean is moving on with his life you're going to try and mess things up for him. You are such a bitch!"

"I am not" wailed Rosie, bursting into tears. Ellie was not impressed. "You needn't try your ol' tactics on me Rosie Maguire, I know you too well" snorted Ellie. "If you mess this up for Sean then you are nothing but a . . . ." Ellie could not think of anything bad enough to call Rosie.

"I know!" wailed Rosie. "I can't help it! Oh, God Ellie, I think I love him." The realisation was too much for Rosie to cope with. Now that Sean was with someone else Rosie wanted him completely. She was paralysed with anxiety and regret.

"I am a stupid cow!"

"Yes you are" said Ellie, "and a rat bag!"

"I know"

"And you eat too much, and you're always sponging cigarettes of me!"

"All right Ellie, I get it!"

"SORRY" said Ellie, sarcastically. "I was just trying to help with the character analysis."

"You were just being a bitch is all" retorted Rosie, but she couldn't help smiling at Ellie's feigned look of contrition.

"So what are you going to do?" asked Ellie, attempting to be more supportive.

"I need to see him" replied Rosie. "I need to know for myself if he is in love with her."

"Well he'll probably be at the disco tonight" said Ellie, trying to be helpful.

"Oh fuckety fuck fuck! I have nothing to wear!" exclaimed Rosie, who was already planning her reunion with Sean and the obliteration of her Spanish rival from his mind and heart.

"Can I borrow . . . ." Rosie did not get to finish her sentence.

"Don't even think of it Rosie Maguire" snipped Ellie. "I am fed up lending you all my clothes. You always stretch them."

"I do not! I am the same size as you!"

"Rosie, the last time you were a size eight, you were eight!" replied Ellie. She was rewarded with a thump on the arm from Rosie, who was becoming quite sensitive about her weight.

The girls cleaned up the dishes together and arranged to meet at Ellie's house that night before the disco. When Ellie left, Rosie immediately transformed into hunt mode, searching for something to borrow from Kate to wear that night. After all, if she was going to compete with the Spanish beauty she would have to make some sort of effort with her appearance. Luckily Kate was away on a holiday with Michael and was not due back until Monday. Finally Rosie settled on a black pencil skirt she had worn to an interview recently and a low cut silver top which Kate had bought the previous year and never worn. *She'll hardly miss it*, thought Rosie, as she dressed that night after showering and putting her make up on. Rosie took more time than normal to dry her hair. She'd had her hair permed the previous month and it was finally starting to relax a bit. It hung in shaggy tendrils around her face and neck. Rosie topped off her outfit with a pair of black stockings and black, suede, stiletto shoes. She had no jewellery to wear. Anne was not home that weekend so, feeling slightly guilty, Rosie opened her jewellery box and took out a pair of silver drop ear-rings. She promised Jesus that if he made sure she didn't get caught she would be extra careful with them. No doubt Jesus was not convinced.

Her toilette complete, Rosie waltzed into the living room and asked her father for a lift into town. Mr Maguire was well used to doing Saturday night taxi runs for his daughters. He often thought about getting himself a proper taxi licence and setting up in business he spent so much time chauffeuring women about. Shane also wanted a lift into town and ran to grab his coat as Rosie waited impatiently by the door for her father to find his car keys. Finally they were on the road and Rosie could not help feeling excited about the evening in front of her. She was slightly worried that Sean might not show up, but she knew that he liked the group *Bagatelle* and she was also sure that there wasn't too many other venue's in town to go to on a Saturday night. There were plenty of pubs in Tullymore but few of them played live music.

It was half past seven when Mr Maguire dropped Rosie at Ellie's house. When Ellie opened the door, Rosie was horrified to see she was in her bathrobe and nowhere near ready to go out. Ellie noticed Rosie's look of horror and told her to relax. The disco did not start until 8.30 and they had plenty of time for a glass or two of cider before going out. Ellie always liked to be fashionably late and make a dramatic entrance wherever she went. Rosie liked to be early to get the best seats (and to be first at the bar). Rosie was comforted by the glass of cider which Ellie produced quickly for her. She was soon feeling mellow and chatted to Ellie as she watched her put her make up on and get ready. Rosie could not help but admire the meticulous way in which Ellie prepared herself. She had already been getting ready for two hours prior to Rosie's arrival and spent a further hour doing her nails and makeup. Her hair was tastefully pulled into an intricate plait at the back of her head.

"I like your bun" said Rosie. Ellie snorted indignantly,

"It's a chignon you moron!" Ellie despaired of Rosie's uncouthness.

"Fancy!" said Rosie, laughing at Ellie's irritation.

When Ellie was ready, she telephoned a taxi to take Rosie and herself to the hotel. Rosie was so excited she could hardly contain herself. It was nearly 9 o'clock when they arrived. Rosie immediately jumped out of the car and began to walk purposefully towards the entrance, leaving Ellie to pay the fare and apologise to the taxi man for her friend's rudeness. They both went into the lounge, and Rosie was ordering two drinks before Ellie had even taken her coat off. Rosie scanned the lounge looking for familiar faces as she waited for the drinks. There was no one of interest in the bar. Ellie chose to sit near the door so that she could see people arriving and, of course, be seen by said arrivees. The band would be playing in the hall next to the lounge. Ellie did not want to go in too early. Rosie set the drinks down and slumped into the seat beside Ellie. She was disappointed Sean was not there. Ellie pointed out that it was far too early for people to start arriving. Rosie offered Ellie a cigarette and they both lit up. Ellie talked about her week in work. Rosie was not really listening. She looked up every time someone entered the bar and sighed deeply when it was not Sean. Ellie was becoming increasingly irritated by Rosie and finally snapped at her,

"You are so rude Rosie, you can't even be bothered pretending to be interested in what I have to say." Rosie was taken aback by the outburst but managed to look sincerely contrite.

"Sorrreeee!" she retorted, "I'm just a bit distracted this evening."

"You're like a cat on a hot tin roof waiting there for Sean to arrive with his new girlfriend so you can destroy his happiness forever" said Ellie spitefully.

"I am not" protested Rosie, knowing there was some truth in what Ellie said. She did want to obliterate the Spanish beauty, but she did not want Sean to be unhappy.

"I do want him to be happy, just not with her. I want him to be happy with me" she said quietly.

"Well I think it will all end in tears, Rosie" said Ellie. "You never wanted Sean before and now that he has a girl you want him to give her up so he can go back to running after you. Either shit or get of the pot Rosie! Sean has the right to get on with his life without you causing him more grief."

Rosie stared at her friend in wonder. She could not understand why Ellie was suddenly so protective of Sean. Was she right? Rosie wondered if she had been leading Sean on all these years. He had never again taken her in his arms and kissed her the way he had that night by the river almost three years ago. He had never again told her that he loved her. He had remained in the background of her life, watching her, as if waiting for her to want him. Now that she did want him Rosie wondered if she could bring herself to admit it to him. She had assumed that he would make the first move. Instead he had found someone else to replace her. She could not bear to think of him loving someone else. Rosie knew that Sean had gone out with girls since Jim's death. They had often joked about their individual bad dates. They had compared notes on who had the worst track record when it came to relationships. Rosie always won that argument. Now there were serious doubts forming in Rosie's mind about her ability to sustain any sort of long term relationship. She believed herself to be damaged goods. She was broken. Not since Jim had her heart been moved to feel anything more than a passing attraction to any man. With Sean it was different. Her feelings for him pre-dated Jim's death. He was so much a part of her life now that, even if she didn't speak to him for weeks, she could always talk to him as if they had never been parted. He knew her better than anyone else and still liked her. She did not have to pretend to be someone else when she was with him. He could always call her on her bullshit and she respected him for that. She loved him.

As Rosie sat pondering the intricacies of her befuddled heart Ellie suddenly nudged her and whispered,
"There's Sean and his new girl." Rosie looked up and her eyes met his almost immediately. He had been looking round the room searching for something. When he saw Rosie, Sean smiled. He quickly took the Spanish one's elbow and directed her towards Rosie and Ellie. Rosie's heart sank. She was gorgeous.
"Hi girls, this is Lola" beamed Sean, "Lola, this is Ellie and Rosie." Ellie proffered her hand to Lola who shook it warmly and said,

"Plezed to meet you". Rosie stammered a quick 'hiya' and shook Lola's hand weakly. "Would you like a drink girls?" asked Sean. Ellie responded before Rosie had time to think, "Of course Sean, we never say no to a drink. Lola do you want to sit down here," she continued, smiling sweetly at Lola and kicking Rosie under the table. Rosie was staring at Lola and making her uncomfortable. The kick brought Rosie to her senses. She recovered her equanimity and managed to move slightly to allow Lola to sit down. Lola was lovely. She and Ellie hit it off immediately. Lola worked in advertising and had met Sean through a mutual friend Kieran, who lived in Barcelona. Sean was visiting Kieran when he had been introduced to Lola. They started dating and kept in touch when Sean returned to Ireland. They had been together for two months. Lola talked incessantly about how great a guy Sean was. She was keen to get to know his family and his friends and appeared to be genuinely interested in anything Ellie had to say. Rosie said very little. The situation was worse than she had ever imagined. This girl was in love with Sean, and watching him interact with her, Rosie could not but notice that he too was in love. It's over she thought to her self. I've lost him and I never even had him.

Rosie excused herself and went to the toilet. She began to shake as soon as she left the lounge, only just managing to reach the privacy of the toilets before breaking into tears. Ellie entered soon after and was not surprised to see the state Rosie was in. Her former hardness was gone and she literally offered Rosie a shoulder to cry on.

"Rosie," she said, "if you really do love Sean then now is the time to show him. You will just have to get him alone and tell him how you feel." The thought petrified Rosie. She was not in the habit of making declarations of love to anyone. "I don't know what to say to him" she whimpered.

"You'll think of something Rosie" said Ellie, "I have never known you to be stuck for words. Just don't say anything stupid or crude. For once in your life try to be an adult about this." *Smug bitch* thought Rosie, but she only nodded in response to Ellie's words. She touched up her make-up and left the toilets with Ellie repeating words of encouragement to her as she went. Rosie felt like a prize fighter entering the ring with her coach at her side.

After finishing their drinks Sean suggested that they all go into the disco so they could get seats together to watch the band. When they entered the dance hall the DJ was just welcoming *Bagatelle* to the stage. Rosie's heart lifted as she heard the first strains of *Trump Card*, one of her favourite songs. She listened to the lyrics while Ellie, Sean and Lola found seats and a table. Ellie offered to get the next round of drinks in, and Lola offered to help carry them. Rosie was left alone with Sean for the first time in months. He looked triumphant. Rosie was uncomfortable. The words of the song continued to run through her head. She noticed Sean singing along.

"I guess this is your trump card Sean" said Rosie, finally plucking up the courage to speak to him.

"What do you mean Rosie?" asked Sean, innocently.

"You know what I mean. I hope you and Lola will be very happy." Sean smiled at her. "Oh, we are both VERY happy" he said, holding Rosie's gaze.

"Are you getting married?" asked Rosie, abandoning all attempts at being coy.

"Yes Rosie, I think I will definitely get married. I am very much in love you know." Rosie looked stricken. "I hope we can still be friends after I'm married, Rosie" he continued, "after all, I cannot imagine my life without you."

"Eye right Sean" snapped Rosie, suddenly losing all her control, "maybe I could baby-sit the brats while you and Lola go out for a night!"

"Well that might be difficult you know if we are living in Barcelona."

"You're moving to Barcelona?" squeaked Rosie. It was the last straw.

"Of course Rosie!" said Sean "Lola has a good job there, and she has family and she doesn't want to live in Ireland. It's too wet."

"She's too wet" muttered Rosie, under her breath.

"Did you say something Rosie?" asked Sean, staring intently into her eyes.

"NO!" exclaimed Rosie, her cheeks colouring.

At that moment Ellie and Lola returned with the drinks. They were both laughing. Rosie felt doubly betrayed. Her best friend was cohorting with the enemy. Lola wanted to dance and playfully begged Sean to join her. He warmly refused saying that he didn't dance to 'girl's songs.' Lola then looked pleadingly at Ellie who was quite happy for the excuse to leave Rosie. It was like sitting beside a wet blanket. Ellie was in the mood for fun. She and Lola quickly made their way to the dance floor, leaving Rosie and Sean alone again. Rosie was stuck for words. She wanted to say something fascinating that would intrigue Sean. She wanted to be flirtatious and sexy. She wanted to tease him, but she was immobilised with trepidation.

"Lola seems very nice" she managed to say, looking at Sean. "Yeah, she's gorgeous!" replied Sean, staring right back at Rosie. Rosie was silent, her face awash in a colour that can only be described as green.

"Are you OK, Rosie?" enquired Sean, looking genuinely concerned.

"I'm fine!" replied Rosie forcing a smile.

"If I didn't know you better I would say that you are jealous, Rosie," stated Sean quietly.

"Oh get over yourself" Rosie said, indignantly. "I am not!"

"So you are not breaking your heart over me then? I must say, I am really disappointed Rosie" said Sean, shaking his head in mock distress, "I always thought that one day you and I would be together and we'd live happily ever after."

"Oh, that would be just lovely" retorted Rosie, "You, me and Lola living in perfect harmony!"

At that moment the band announced that they were going to slow things down. The opening bars of *Second Violin* caught Rosie's attention. It was another one of her favourite songs,

"I'm nobody's second violin, Sean" she stated flatly, with as much dignity as she could muster. Sean watched her closely as she stood up and lifted her handbag and coat. Rosie could no longer stand the tension. She wanted to go home so she could lick her wounds in private.

"Dance with me Rosie" said Sean. It was not a request. As if in a trance, Rosie put her coat and bag down, and took Sean's outstretched hand. They walked to the dance floor and Sean placed his hands around Rosie's waist, pulling her closer than was strictly necessary. As the song played on Rosie's trance like state deepened. She did not want the dance to end. She did not want Sean to move away from her. She wanted to stay in his arms, protected and safe forever. The song ended. Sean slowly peeled Rosie away from him. Holding her at arms length he smiled at her.

"I love you Rosie" he said.

"Really?" questioned Rosie in disbelief, "but I thought you and Lola were getting married." Sean smiled at her. Taking Rosie by the hand he led her outside into the garden at the back of the hotel. They sat down on a garden bench before Sean spoke again.

"Lola IS getting married, Rosie . . . . to my mate Kieran. He lives in Barcelona. When I was staying there Lola and I became friends. She asked me to help her make Kieran jealous. She was in love with him but he didn't seem to notice. The plan worked. After I showed an interest in Lola, Kieran decided that he could live without her and proposed. They're getting married next year. I'm the best man." Rosie remained speechless while she absorbed the information.

"Hold on then!" she said, eventually, "then why is Lola here with you?"

"*Quid Pro Quo!*" Sean said laughing.

"You total bollocks!" gasped Rosie, realisation suddenly dawning on her.

"You mean you were just trying to make me jealous?"

"Did it work, Rosie?" asked Sean, almost apologetically.

"I may well hate your forever but I have to admit it worked . . . . a wee bit!" laughed Rosie. Sean looked relieved.

"Do you love me?" he asked, suddenly becoming nervous. Rosie thought about it for a moment. She remembered the love she had felt for Jim. She did not feel like that about Sean. It was different. She could tell him anything. He had seen her at her worst. He knew who she was. She had never been anything other than one hundred per cent Rosie when she was with him, and he still loved her.

"Yes, I love you" she said quietly. Sean's eyes brightened. He looked relieved.

"Will you be my girlfriend?" he asked.

"I guess somebody has to be!" laughed Rosie. At that moment Sean leaned over and took her in his arms. The kiss lasted for a very long time. Rosie was almost breathless when Sean released her. *Wow*, she thought, *I could get used to that.*

As they walked back towards the entrance of the hotel Sean put his arm around Rosie's waist. It felt good there. Rosie's head began to fill with possibilities. She pictured herself and Sean making love. She saw them travelling the world together. She saw them having children and growing old together. Mostly though, Rosie longed for the disco to end so she could be alone with Sean. She also wanted to get to the Chinese takeaway beside the hotel before everyone else. After all, falling in love was extremely draining, and Rosie's earlier (albeit brief) loss of appetite had rendered her ravenous. Now that she had secured her Sean, Rosie knew in her heart that she would never be hungry again.

The End

Lightning Source UK Ltd.
Milton Keynes UK
UKOW040827200613

212557UK00001B/14/P